Alice's Journey Beyond the Moon

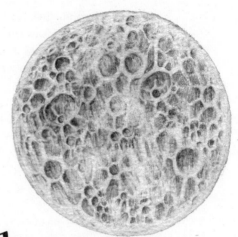

Alice's Journey Beyond the Moon

Edited and annotated by R.J. Carter

Illustrated by Lucy Wright

First published in England in 2004 by
Telos Publishing Ltd
61 Elgar Avenue, Tolworth, Surrey, KT5 9JP, England
www.telos.co.uk

Telos Publishing Ltd values feedback.
Please e-mail us with any comments you may have about this book to: feedback@telos.co.uk

ISBN: 1-903889-76-6 (paperback)
Alice's Journey Beyond the Moon © 2004 R. J. Carter.
Illustrations © 2004 Lucy Wright

ISBN: 1-903889-77-4 (deluxe hardback)
Alice's Journey Beyond the Moon © 2004 R. J. Carter.
Illustrations © 2004 Lucy Wright

The moral rights of the author have been asserted.

Internal design, typesetting and layout by ATB Publishing Inc.
www.atbpublishing.com

Printed in India
Hardback bound in the UK by Antony Rowe Ltd

1 2 3 4 5 6 7 8 9 10 11 12 13 14 15

British Library Cataloguing in Publication Data.
A catalogue record for this book is available from the British Library.

To Bobbie, who endures me without often understanding why.

Acknowledgements

The author would like to thank...

Neil Gaiman, who left the title lying about in the Library of Dreams, where just about anyone could nick it, so that's hardly my fault, is it?

Mark Israel of the Lewis Carroll Society, for navigating the ship through temporal anomalies and other boojums of language.

Sean Klein, Georgiana Lee, Terri Brown-Davidson, Thea Atkinson, Kevin Dolgin and others who will undoubtedly remind me I forgot them, for providing critiques along the way – and Francis Ford Coppola for providing them a place to do so.

Troy Riser, for showing me the rabbit hole.

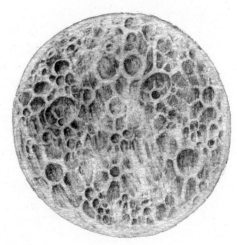

Foreword

I seldom read introductions. I prefer to skip straight to the story proper. If you are of a like mind, feel free to do the same. I assure you, you'll engender no ill will from me. Run along. Really, it's fine. We'll catch up with you later. Just wait for us on the page that begins 'Dedication'.

Those of you still here may find this information of some enhancement to the tale you are about to read.

As one who takes pleasure in all things Carrollian, I was overjoyed with the discovery (during recent renovations of the library at Christ Church, Oxford) of several papers authored by the Reverend Charles Lutwidge Dodgson. They had seemingly fallen behind a large wooden shelf and had remained lost there for more than a century. Among the letters, memoranda, and sundry doodles, was this manuscript: an unpublished Alice story!

The story was never referenced in any of Carroll's diary entries, which is why it came as such a completely unexpected surprise. Though we have done our best to annotate this particular story, it may be that there are many mysteries in the manuscript left unsolved (if not, indeed, unnoticed.) However, that which we have been able to clarify has been noted, and it is these annotations (as well as the manuscript itself, of course) that we now present to you, fully illustrated in a manner of which we are sure the great author would have approved.

In her previous incarnations, Alice travelled *under* the ground and *through* a looking glass. She rounds out her adventures in this story with a trip *beyond* the moon.

So let us now rejoin our earlier companions, at the start of our wonderful journey. They're waiting for us just over on the next page.

R. J. Carter

Dedication

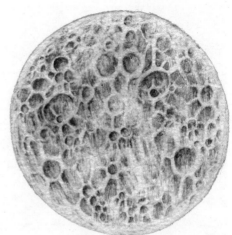

To a child no longer, in memory of golden summer yesterdays, and with God's eternal blessings on all your to-morrows.

A spark lit on that golden day[1]
Lingers yet upon my eye.
In visions, Alice, still at play,
Child of dreams and fantasy[2].

Ere some scholar, being clever,
Peers behind these purple pages,[3]
Here is found but fondness, ever
Ageless though the author ages.

Reflecting on those wondrous days,
Girds me 'gainst despair and gloom.
Reveries stave off malaise
E'en unto my very tomb.

Alice, though in womanhood,
Vestal days all left behind,
Ever wanders tulgy wood,
Snarks and Jabberwocks to find.

1 The stanzas acrostically spell ALICE P. HARGREAVES, indicating the story was written during or after 1880. Alice Liddell was wed to Reginald Hargreaves on 15 September 1880. The story may have been intended as a wedding present, although whether the manuscript was lost or purposely held back is unknown.

2 Compare with:
    I'm the Dean of Christ
        Church; – Sir
    There's my wife, look
        well at her.
    She's the Broad and I'm
        the High:
    We're the University.
Dean Liddell reportedly pronounced 'university' as 'universitie', hence the rhyme with 'high'. *Lewis Carroll: A Biography.* Donald Thomas. 1996. (Carroll also uses this style in the first two lines of the closing poem to *Through The Looking-Glass.*)

3 In 1871, Carroll switched from using black ink to purple, which he used until 1891, when he changed back to black. IBID.

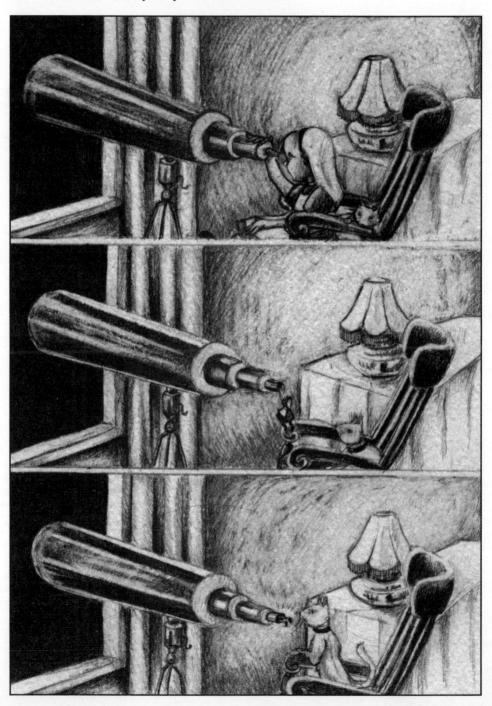

Chapter 1.

From the Parlour to the Moon

Alice sat alone in the parlour, curled up in the big chair with her cat, Snowball. The grown-ups had dispersed for the time being – the men to the study for brandy and cigars, the ladies to the sitting room – leaving Alice unattended with the monstrous telescope, which was aimed out the large open windows toward the full moon. The telescope had been the centre of all attention earlier, with all the grownups peering through its eyepiece and making little "ooh"s and "ah"s and talking about how wonderful and awe-inspiring it would be when the eclipse occurred. Alice ventured to ask what an eclipse was, and how it could make the moon disappear, and how the moon might come back afterwards, but the matter was never quite explained to her satisfaction.[4]

"They say that the moon is made of green cheese," said Alice, stroking the lazy cat's belly. "Do you believe that, Snowball? Father says it's nothing more than a great white stone[5], and I suppose I ought to believe him; but really, how can one be sure without ever having been there?" Alice wondered how far

4 This would place the events of this story on August 13, 1859, nearly nine months after the events of *Through The Looking-Glass*. The date was that of one of the longest lunar eclipses in history. The fictional Alice would have been 8 years old.

5 Carroll recorded particularly good days in his diary as being marked "with a white stone," adopting the Roman method of marking good days or bad days on the calendar with white chalk or charcoal. White stone days were, almost without exception, days on which he had the opportunity to make the acquaintance of some young girl.

exactly it might be to the moon. She had read in a book somewhere that the moon was quite far away, and much larger than it appeared, but she couldn't recall anything specific. She decided it had to be closer than Russia ("For I can see the moon quite well from here, and I can't see any of Russia at all, even with the telescope," she said to the cat), and farther away than London or Bath (but not too much farther, as the moon came up just on the other side of the one, and went down slightly beyond the other). Which, as best as Alice could calculate, put it comfortably around forty-two miles.[6]

As Alice looked at the moon through the open window, she thought she spied a brief sparkle, such as one might see in the quick glint of a diamond when it catches the light just so. "Oh! Did you see that, Snowball?" Alice asked. "I wonder what that was. Perhaps if I look through the telescope, I should be able to see it again, and more clearly."

Alice peered through the eyepiece and turned the knobs the way she had seen the others doing earlier. "I cannot understand why this device works," said Alice, as the moon grew larger and larger in her sight. "By turning these knobs, one can actually bring the moon closer! Look – now it's only perhaps a few miles away. And now it's no further than Miss Prickett's quarters!"

Alice continued playing with the telescope, bringing the moon larger and larger into view. "Goodness!" thought Alice, "If I persist, surely the moon will soon bump right against the roof!" But she did continue to turn the knobs, and the moon continued to grow.

"And do you know, Snowball," she said,

6 Another instance of Carroll's fascination with the number 42, *q.v.* the King's rule in *Alice's Adventures In Wonderland* ('Alice's Evidence'). In *The Hunting of the Snark*, reference is made to a 'Rule 42', (in the preface) and the baker arrives on the ship with forty-two boxes (in "Fit 1").

although the cat was ignoring her quite well, "that if one looks through the far end of the telescope, it makes things look very small and far away? Why, I suppose by now I must look quite tiny to whoever is on the moon looking back at me. Here am I, making the moon ever larger, and they must be thinking, 'Where is Alice? She was just there, waving at us, and now she's shrunk quite out of view!'"

And then Alice discovered that the telescope was indeed making her smaller (or perhaps the telescope was getting larger), for suddenly she found it quite easy to slip into the eyepiece of the telescope. "Oh!" she cried. "I have telescoped myself! I could crawl all the way up and pop right out the other end! And I suppose I must come out the other end, if I should ever want to be my right size again."

And crawl she did, the moon growing slowly closer all the while. It seemed that she was crawling for a very long time, and Alice began to wonder if the moon was perhaps much farther away than she had previously thought.

But just when Alice had crawled so much that she was quite out of breath ("Really," she thought, huffing and puffing, "there must be an easier way found to get to the moon. Perhaps someone ought to build a railway?"), she suddenly found that she was no longer climbing *up* the slope, but was rather sliding *down* it[7], going faster (and getting larger) the entire time, until – Pop! she flew out the far end and landed quite rough and tumble on the moon.

"Oh!" Alice exclaimed, looking about. "Well, it's not all that much to look at, I suppose. All

7 In *Sylvie and Bruno*, Carroll wrote of gravity-powered trains that worked on the principle of going down and then up, yet always going in a straight line. Alice's climb and slide uses this logic in reverse when she reaches the half-way point between the Earth and the moon.

grey and spongy, and not made out of green cheese at all!"

"You mean to say, 'It's not all made out of green cheese.'" Alice turned about and saw a dappled mare, its head drooped and its eyelids languid, standing without bit or bridle or saddle. "It's most of the same words, I know, but the way you arranged them was all wrong. There are bits and pieces that are made of green cheese. The rest is made up of cheddar, Camembert, Roquefort, bleu and some others that even I ca'n't abide the smell of."

"Oh, I beg your pardon," Alice said, not realising there were so many kinds of cheese of which she was unaware.

"No need to beg," the mare replied. "And I doubt you would be any good at it, at any rate. You haven't the proper look for the job.[8] Appearances are important to being successful, you know. But the fact of the matter is that that there are many other kinds of cheese than the green variety." The mare yawned, then shook its muzzle. "Why, just to your left is a great mound of aging cheese that will probably be harvested soon."

Alice looked about and saw what looked to her to be an anthill, only nearly as tall as herself and filled with many holes. Curious, she broke off a small bit and tasted it, and found it quite sharp but not at all indigestible. "What sort of cheese is this?" she asked.

The mare came awake with a jerk (for it had dozed off while Alice was nibbling). "I believe I told you," it said. "It's aging cheese."

This seemed rather silly to Alice, for she knew at least enough about cheese to know that all cheese had to be aged before it could rightly be called cheese. She popped the

8 One of Carroll's most famous photographs of Alice shows her dressed as a beggar girl.

remaining bit into her mouth and turned to break off some more.

But the little pile of cheese was smaller than before, or so it seemed, standing now only as high as Alice's waist. "I'm sure it was taller than this a moment ago," she thought, as she ate another piece. "I do wish there were more of it, though. It's quite good, and I am still a little hungry. I wonder if – Oh!" (for when she reached out again, she saw that her hands were wrinkled). She inspected her hands with great care before bringing them to her cheeks, only to learn that they were also shrivelled. Indeed, upon examination, she determined that she had somehow become an old woman. "Goodness," she said to herself. "I must have been standing here ever so long! I didn't even realise I was getting older. Oh, I must have missed quite a number of birthday parties." And she sat on a boulder of hard cheese and quietly lamented over all the cake she had never eaten and all the presents she had never opened.

"I do wish you'd be quieter," the horse said, yawning so wide that Alice could count all of its teeth (although she did not do so, for she felt it was rude to look a horse in the mouth – or so she seemed to remember having heard somewhere or other).

"Quiet?" Alice asked indignantly. "But I haven't said a thing!"

"Well then, stop thinking quite so loudly," the horse said. "I'm trying to get some sleep."

Alice began to protest that she was thinking as quietly as she knew how, but she was interrupted.

"Sleep?" The voice was so shrill as to make Alice grit her teeth, which she dared not do too tightly, for they were old and loose and ready to fall out! "Sleep? Plenty of time to sleep when you've done being awake!"[9] Alice saw that the voice's owner was a very curious-looking old woman, dressed in mouldy tatters and cobwebs. She did, however, have an odd sort of crown upon her head, on which were engraved several star shapes, and so Alice supposed her to be a Queen of some sort despite her humble raiment. She walked with a rather pronounced limp, and her face was all drawn up as though she ever ate only lemons and pickles and drank only persimmon juice with alum.

"She's certainly a very poor sort of Queen," Alice thought, as she watched her approach. She was rather reminded of an old rhyme, and she endeavoured to repeat it:

Walking in the moon dust,
In her robe and crown,
I saw Missus Spiderwebs,
With her dour frown,
Full of moans, full of moans,
Crotchety and creased,
How shall her knees stop their groans,
If they are not greased?[10]

"That's not right, though," said Alice, her own old knees groaning just a little. "I'm quite sure it was meant to be about a cat. I shall have to ask Snowball when I get home."

"Where is our cart? Where is our horseman?" the Queen screeched. "I say, it's getting so one has to do everything for oneself, and that's certain to be the downfall of those as ca'n't do for anybody!"

Alice looked about and saw a very small wooden wheelbarrow nearby, with a harness

9 Carroll was a notorious insomniac. He often stayed awake nights developing logical and mathematical solutions to an odd assortment of puzzles, which he documented in *Pillow Problems*.

10 The verse parodies the first stanza of an old nursery rhyme, 'Mother Tabbyskins'. The original went as follows:
   Sitting in the garden, in
      her cloak and hat,
   I saw Mother Tabbyskins,
      the real old cat,
   Very old, very old, crumplety and lame,
   Teaching kittens how to
      scold, is it not a shame?

attached. "Perhaps this is the cart she is looking for," thought Alice.

"You there!" said the Queen to Alice. "Get about your task! This horse isn't at all ready to transport."

"She must want me to harness this cart to the horse," Alice said to herself. "Well, I shall try, but I've never managed such a contrivance before, and never have I been so feeble."

Alice wheeled the cart over to the horse and began looping the harness over the horse's muzzle. The horse for its part was too slumberous to resist, and Alice was glad for that bit of luck. The Queen stayed close at hand, eyeing Alice suspiciously as she did her best to attach beast to barrow.

"That is all wrong!" the Queen scolded. "Wrong! Wrong! Wrong! You're placing the – And now you've put the rudder where the bowsprit – !" And she continued to sputter and haul Alice over the coals until, in a fit of utter frustration, she took the harness and reins from Alice. "Useless," she muttered. "Utterly useless." And she set about looping the harness around the horse's fetlocks and cannons in all manner of knots, until the poor thing's hocks were drawn up right into its elbows, and Alice was certain the horse would not be able to take even a single step without falling over. Which bothered the horse not in the least, for the sleepy beast had no intention of making any movement beyond that required for a simple snore.

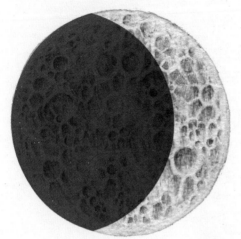

Chapter II.

Philosophy and Horse Sense

The horse yawned again, barely able to stay awake despite its awkward state, and made not even the slightest pretence at pulling the contraption.[11] If the Queen noticed, she made no mention of it. Instead, she turned her attention toward Alice.

"So then," she said. "State your business here in our kingdom. Be quick about it now! Don't stammer!"

"I have no business here, your Majesty," Alice said as graciously as she could. "I hadn't even the intention of coming here, truthfully. It's only that the telescope was looking at the moon, and I ..."

"Looking at the moon!" the Queen gasped. "Spying on us, we should think! A nosy old woman eager to get her hands on the riches of our kingdom."

Alice looked about at the ramshackle carriage and the shabbiness of the Queen's attire. "If there are riches to be had here, they are certainly well hidden," thought Alice. Then she said aloud, "I'm not an old woman. I'm a little girl, and I was only looking, not spying at all," feeling completely justified that

11 There has been some debate as to whether or not this 'tranquil mare' was an unwritten pun on Mare Tranquilis, or 'Sea of Tranquillity'.

one activity in no way implied the other.

"Humph," said the Queen, eyeing her up and down. "Next you'll be telling us stroking is not the same as striking, or that there's a difference between being liberal and being literal." She folded her arms across her chest, haughtily. "You may as well try to convince us that falling is unlike flying."

Alice fell silent, for while she wanted to explain that there was more than a letter or two of difference in all those things, she felt it would do no good to argue.

"Of all the nerve," the Queen went on, although a bit more calmly than before. "What ever were you thinking?"

"I'm sure I wasn't thinking anything at all," said Alice.

"Nothing at all?" the Queen said. "Quite shocking! Quite! You must have had some thought in your head at the time, else you must have been asleep. Or perhaps you were dead?"

"I'm quite certain I wasn't dead," said Alice. "And I don't think I was asleep. I remember I was talking to Snowball – she's a very darling cat, really, although she tends to scratch at the chair when she shouldn't – and the telescope was there, and suddenly I was here. It's really a very strange thing to be here, and I'm quite sure if I thought anything at all, it shouldn't be anything so curious that it should carry me to the moon."

"Pish tosh!" the Queen said. "There is nothing so strange or implausible to think about that someone else hasn't already thought it up at one time or another."

"Oh, I do wish I hadn't eaten that aging cheese," said Alice.

"What!" the Queen cried, aghast. "You're not only a spy, but a thief as well! We shall have you locked up, we shall, see if we don't!"

The mare clumped one hoof against the ground, lazily, and began to lean to one side. "I don't know about you, but I always feel younger whenever I have a nice long drink of ginger beer," it said, sleepily.

The Queen gave no notice to the mare, but Alice looked about, as though she might find a bottle of ginger beer lying about that she might not have noticed earlier.

As luck would have it, there was indeed a bottle of ginger beer – several bottles, in fact – just beneath the carriage seat. With a trembling hand, Alice took one of the bottles, pulled the stopper, and took a long swig of the sweet liquid inside. She kept drinking until the last golden drop had trickled into her mouth, and when she looked at herself again, she saw she was back to her proper age. "I'm still a bit thirsty," she thought, "but I'm sure it wouldn't do to drink another bottle. Goodness knows I shouldn't wish to become younger than I am already. Imagine, having to endure all those lessons again!"

"Hurry it up!" the Queen bellowed at the mare, heedless of Alice's changes. "We shall never get there on time at this rate. We may not have some gaudy golden chariot and a fine team of stallions like those of a certain braggart we know who rules the sun, but we refuse to be treated this shabbily! Oh, when we arrive, we are going to have our stable hands put some good sense into this awful beast."

The horse yawned. "I sha'n't be needing that, thank you. I have enough already."

"That must be what people mean by horse

sense," thought Alice, who had always wondered if horses truly had sense or whether it was just a silly phrase uttered by grown-ups.

"Surely you haven't," the Queen said.

"I have," the horse insisted. "Just enough. She has enough. You have enough. Everyone has enough good sense. They must, for even those most difficult to please in all other matters," (and here the tired old mare cut her eyes sharply at the Queen), "do not commonly desire more of it than they already possess."

"Poppycock!" said the Queen. "Tell us," she said to Alice, "have you all the good sense you need, dear child?" And she smiled so widely and with so much sugar that the wrinkles on her cheeks bunched together into such an arrangement that Alice couldn't tell whether the facial gesture was a friendly one or not.

Alice pondered if she was as full of good sense as the horse had said. She remembered that she was to come indoors when it began raining, and that she should never speak loudly at the table during breakfast. However, just the other day she had put her left shoe on her right foot, so perhaps she could still use more good sense than she had. Still, she felt sorry for the horse, and she was sure she didn't care much for the Queen at all.

"Come, come," the Queen said, snappishly. "Are you full up on all the good sense you need, then?"

"I think," said Alice. "I am. What I mean is – " But the Queen interrupted, gesticulating nervously.

"Hush hush hush!" she whispered, quite panicked. "One ought never put Descartes before a horse."

But it was too late.[12] "Don't mind if I do," said the sleepy old nag, who then stepped out of the loops of the harness and managed to squeeze into the back of the cart. Within an instant, she was quickly snoring, and would not wake no matter how much Alice cajoled or the Queen threatened until, finally, Alice was forced to pull the cart herself.

12 Too late, indeed! The Queen mistakes Alice's statements as the famous "I think, therefore I am," posited by Rene Descartes. But the Queen has already paraphrased Descartes twice herself, and the horse's statement about good sense is also taken from the writings of the French philosopher.

Chapter III.

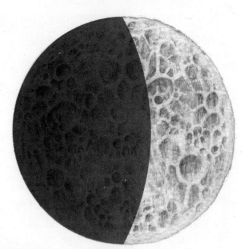

Soldiers
& Sentinels

A lice hauled the carriage, much like a Chinaman[13] at a rickshaw, until she was walking through a great field of stones, set in rows as far as the eye could see.

"This is as far as I go," said Alice, dropping the handles and letting them fall to the ground. "If either of you wants to continue, someone else is going to have to take over pulling." But when Alice turned around, both the horse and the Queen were gone.

"Well, I do wish they had had the good manners to tell me they were leaving," Alice thought, indignantly. "I might well have left off hauling this awful thing about several miles ago."

Alice read aloud the inscription on the nearest stone:

MEMENTO MORI
HER MOST REGAL MAJESTY
REGINA LUNAE
QUEEN OF THE MOON
ETIAM DICET IUCUNDE TERRIS
HESTERNIS[14]

13 Alice Liddell had been a Chinaman before, in one of Carroll's photographs.

14 "Even yet she speaks pleasantly from yesterday's world," or words to that effect. Carroll inserts another acrostic here as well: EDITH. Edith Liddell was Alice's younger sister, who died in 1876 of appendicitis.

"Oh dear," said Alice. "That *was* sudden. I didn't even know she was ill. Well, I suppose I shall have to forgive her rudeness, for one really ca'n't control when one is going to die, after all."

"She can," said a voice behind her.

Alice turned to see a wood louse, as large as she, wearing a soldier's uniform that was all done in pink, except for a thin white sash at the waist.

"She does it all the time," came another voice, from the direction Alice had just been facing. She turned again to see another wood louse, outfitted like the first, only all in brown, with a white cummerbund about its middle.

"Here now, you," said the first soldier wood louse to the second. "You won't get in this way! Off with you!" And it rolled itself into a large pink ball and set itself at the other soldier with such fury that the brown wood louse was knocked to the ground,whereupon it too curled into a tight little ball, and was sent rolling over the hill and out of sight. ("Very like a pink croquet ball knocking a brown one out of play," thought Alice.)

"He's right, you know," said the pink wood louse soldier, brushing the dust from his hands. "She does do it all the time."

"I know I shouldn't wish to try it," said Alice.

"It's easy as eating pie!" the soldier said dismissively. "Once you get it out of the way, that is[15]. But she really oughtn't to enjoy it so much."

"Surely you haven't had time or opportunity to bury her, let alone hold a proper funeral." Alice rather regretted missing the funeral, for she was certain she would have

15 In 1898, Carroll repeated this sentiment in a letter to his sister, Louisa, in which he writes: "I sometimes think what a grand thing it will be to be able to say to oneself, 'Death is *over* now; there is not *that* experience to be faced again.'" *The Life and Letters of Lewis Carroll*. Stuart Dodgson Collingwood. 1898.

been able to say a few kind words, even if she did have to make them up.

"No one dares bury[16] her," he said. "She'll only return in a few days anyhow, and she'd be quite cross at the imposition of having to dust herself off."

Alice wanted to ask where the Queen went if she was dead and not buried, but feared that she might actually learn the answer. She looked down at the monument for the Queen, and then noticed the stone next to it was similarly inscribed, but with a different date. Indeed, a closer inspection revealed that every stone in the entire garden was a memorial to that same personage.

"We're obligated to erect a stone each time," the soldier said with a sigh, kicking tentatively at one of the multiple monuments. "They're her graves[17], after all, even if she chooses not to lie in them. Little[18] as you are, I shouldn't expect you to understand that. When your Mays become Septembers, you'll know better.[19] Still, it does seem such a waste at times." He bent down and polished the stone with a cloth he pulled from one of his many pockets. "And the upkeep! They have to be new, and we must wax them constantly, lest their lustre should ever wane (and oh, but she'd have a fit if that ever happened!). But, I say," he said, straightening and putting the cloth back away, "we haven't been properly introduced. How do you do?"

"How do you do?" asked Alice.

The wood louse peered at Alice, thoughtfully. "That's an appropriate response," he said finally, "and an even better repeating. But it is not, as answers go, a very good one."

16 Carroll's father was the curate of Daresbury, in Cheshire, where Carroll spent his earliest years.

17 'Hargreaves', perhaps?

18 If the assumption in footnote 17 is correct, then this would be 'Liddell'. Some have thought this to mean that Alice was still 'Liddell' at the time of the writing, but it is more likely Carroll was simply making a wordplay on her maiden name.

19 Alice's birthday was in May, her wedding anniversary in September.

"What do you mean?" asked Alice, for she was quite sure she had observed every proper rule of etiquette for formally greeting someone.

"I mean that I asked you a question, and you asked me the same question back," said the wood louse. "If I had asked you, 'Where did you place your shoes?' you might be expected to say 'In the aquarium,' or, 'Behind the cupboard,' or even, 'On my ears.' You wouldn't stupidly echo my query back to me, would you?"

Alice considered this and, after a little while of the wood louse's impatiently tapping one foot while waiting for her to reply, decided the wisest course of action would be to agree.

"Then let's begin again," the wood louse said. "How do you do?"

"I do very well, thank you," said Alice politely.

"What do you do very well?" he asked, leaning in to inspect her more closely.

Now Alice was thoroughly confused. "I'm afraid I don't understand what it is you wish me to say," she said.

"You said you do very well," the wood louse said. "Well then, what is it that you do very well? Take me, for instance. I'm the Pink Sentinel. I stand here and guard the door to this castle, so that enemy soldiers cannot pass. I shouldn't let you pass either, were you to try, so please don't. I'm sure I shouldn't like to take you prisoner."[20]

"I'm sure I should not like that either," Alice said. She looked past the wood louse and noticed, for the first time, that there was behind him an arched gateway and, even farther back, a thin stone tower. ("It's not

20 Carroll invented 'Croquet Castles', a twist on the standard game, and published it in *Aunt Judy's Magazine* in August 1867 (first published anonymously in 1863). The game involved two balls (a soldier and a sentinel) for each of four players, who – while not stated outright – could rightly be called kings and queens, as each had a castle, or peg.

much of a castle," thought Alice. "It's hardly more than a turret.")

The wood louse suddenly leaned over and grasped its knees (or one pair of them) and began panting so heavily that Alice suddenly found herself concerned for the poor thing's health.

"I shall be fine," he said between breaths. "It's only that I'm winded from swatting away that awful brown soldier."

"Well then," thought Alice, "he's certainly in no condition to be taking anyone prisoner just now." And she stepped through the gate and ran toward the tower.

"Wait!" wheezed the wood louse. "You ca'n't! I ca'n't take two![21] Oh, dash it all!" And he ran after Alice as best he could, but he had yet to recover from his prior battle and, as Alice put more and more distance between them, he gave up the chase and sat on a large flat rock to catch his breath.

As she neared the tower, Alice heard the familiar screeching voice of the Queen. "Sentinel!" she crowed, demandingly. "Where are you? Why is the gate unguarded?"

"So she does come back after all," thought Alice. "Just as the wood louse said. Well, I suppose no one has to stay *anywhere* for ever.[22]"

21 'Taking two' is terminology used in croquet. The pink wood louse had not gone through a hoop or touched a peg since battling off the brown wood louse. Therefore he could not go after Alice.

22 When he died, an unpublished essay of Carroll's on 'Eternal Punishment' was found. It was a subject he had discussed before in his letters. Carroll had come to believe that to punish humans eternally for a temporal sin was wrong, and a just God would not permit it. He believed that the Bible had been mistranslated, his argument being that the Greek word, αἰών, when describing punishment, did not mean 'eternal'. *Lewis Carroll: A Biography*. Donald Thomas. 1996.

Chapter IV.

The Man in the Moon

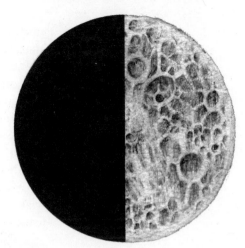

Alice stood before the great tower. In the courtyard there was a large sundial, beneath which cavorted creatures that seemed to Alice to be part badger, part lizard, and part corkscrew. They spun about in such a manner that Alice was sure she should become dizzy were she to continue watching them, and those that weren't running about were darting under and out of the large sundial, or dining on bits of rock.

"What curious little beasts!" thought Alice. "But I'm sure I've heard tell of them somewhere. I think they're called borogoves, or mome raths, or some such thing.[23]"

Alice knocked upon the door.

"Hallo then!" came a voice from inside. "Who is it? What do you want? I am an aged, aged man[24], and ca'n't be subjected to such excitement at this late hour!"

"My name is Alice," she said. "I only want to come in the tower."

A little door opened within the greater door, and Alice saw the most peculiar person looking out at her. His head was completely bald and pale, although the cheeks were

23 The creatures are toves, as described by Humpty Dumpty in *Through the Looking-Glass*. Dumpty said the creatures eat mostly cheese, so we can assume that the portion of the moon Alice has now ventured into is made – if not of green cheese – then certainly of some variety, as the toves are eating what Alice assumes to be rocks.

24 Carroll often referred to himself in letters to his child friends as "the aged, aged man," or "AAM" for short. As with the Dodo and the White Knight, Carroll inserts himself as a character in the story.

mottled with a bit of greyness. But more than that, the man's head had such a roundness and bigness to it, as did his eyes, which were magnified greatly by the great round spectacles he wore, and beamed down at her, blinking[25]. "So you are, and so you do," the man said. "Now go away." And he hastily slammed the door shut.

Alice turned the doorknob and, finding the door to be unlocked, boldly entered. "I only wish to come inside away from those fearsome-looking creatures," she said.

"The toves?" said the old man. "They sha'n't harm you. Odd that they should be out and about at this time. It's far past brillig. You have seen toves before, haven't you, dear?"

Alice conceded that she had not, but that she had once had them described to her by Humpty Dumpty. Indeed, she found that the elderly gentleman quite reminded her of the egg-shaped fellow. His head was extraordinarily large, and just as round no matter what angle you viewed it from. However, the body that held it up was so thin and frail that Alice could not fathom how it could support such a head. "I suppose," she thought, "that his head must be very light." And indeed, it did appear to give off a bit of brilliance all its own.

The old man cleared his throat and gave Alice a doubtful look. "Quite impossible. Mr Dumpty is a dear friend of mine, and I know quite well that he detests little girls. I should go and ask him to put the lie to your tale, but he is taking holiday on the Isle of Eigg, where he is to sing[26] for the Scots. He's a fine baritone, you know – voice like a hypotemuse!"

"A hypotemuse?" Alice asked.

25 "... from which his mild eyes beamed on us through a gigantic pair of spectacles." Carroll's description of Mein Herr in a chapter called 'The Man in the Moon', from *Sylvie and Bruno*.

26 The white singing sands are found on the Isle of Eigg, off the western coast of Scotland. They produce a variety of musical tones when touched or walked upon, due to the structure of the grains.

The old man looked at her with such pity, and Alice thought he must find her incredibly stupid. He squatted down so that his eyes were on a level with hers (or as near as he could get them with a head so large).

"A hypotemuse," he explained slowly, "is a great beast with an extremely thick hide. They have the most mellifluous bellow."

"They sing, then?" asked Alice.

"When they are rightly inclined[27]," the gentleman said. "But, goodness! You must be starving. I'll wager you'd like some crescents! My cook, Hayah," (he said it to rhyme with 'payor') "has just finished baking a batch. Actually, I believe he made them to shingle the roof, but I'm sure he can spare a few for us. And he always has a hot kettle ready. I shan't be a moment."

Left alone, Alice took stock of her surroundings ("For it would never do not to know where one is at," she thought, "particularly if a fire or some other dreadful event were to occur.") She noticed that the ceiling of the room was papered from corner to corner with calendar pages and, upon closer inspection, that the pages were all February. "They're not even from the same year," thought Alice. "There's one from this year. And there's one from a hundred years ago. And there's one I'm sure they shouldn't be printing for another dozen years."

She walked slowly about the room, her head craned back looking up at pages. "I seem to recall there was a rather important poem that mentioned February. I wonder if I can remember it. Let's see …" And she closed her eyes and endeavoured to repeat it:

Twenty-eight days hath February,

27 A 'hypotenuse' is, of course, the inclined side of a right angle triangle, opposite the right angle.

February, February, and February.
All the rest have eight and a score,
Excepting February – which by rights,
Hath days to fill up two fortnights.[28]

"Oh, I'm certain that's not right," Alice fretted. And as she tried to remember again the proper words, she quite forgot to look where she was going and backed into the funny little man, who had just entered with a tray of tea and crescents.

"Who are y-y-you?" he asked, blinking through his enormous glasses in surprise and rattling the tray so that Alice was quite sure he was going to drop the entire thing.

"If it pleases you, sir, my name is Alice," she said, and she wondered if she had forgotten to introduce herself earlier.

"It puh-puh-pleases me not at all," the man sputtered. "You shouldn't buh-be here, alone like th-this! Unchaperoned! Wh-wh-why, what would Mrs G-Grundy say? No, no, you mu-must leave at once!" And he dropped the tray on the nearest surface, then covered his eyes with his hands and ran out with such blind haste that he rapped his forehead quite hard against the door as he left.

"Well, how rude," Alice thought. "If he didn't want me here, he shouldn't have allowed me in. And he certainly needn't have offered me anything to eat."

But just as Alice was standing to leave, the man entered once again, looking a bit perplexed and rubbing a slightly swollen bruise on his forehead.

"Now where did I put that ... Ah, there they are!" he said, upon spying the tray. "How odd, I don't remember seeing them here when

28 The original nursery rhyme has many forms. The one being parodied here seems to be the version from *The Return from Parnassus*, in 1606. It reads:

Thirty days hath September,
April, June and November;
All the rest have thirty-one,
Excepting leap-year – that's
the time,
When February's days are
twenty-nine.

I left."

"But you brought them in only a moment ago," said Alice, very puzzled at the man's behaviour.

"Did I?" he asked. "How curious!"

"Or someone who looked like you, at the very least."

"Ah, well, that explains it," he said, with some chagrin. "*He* was here."

"For a moment I half-believed he was you," said Alice.

"He is I," said the man. "That is to say, I am he. Only I shouldn't wish to be he just now, and we hardly ever choose to be each other at the same time. He's a dodgy old man, and I do hope he doesn't return to bother you before we've had our tea."[29]

As he spoke, he poured the tea into the three cups, setting one before Alice, one in front of an empty chair, and the third he kept for himself.

"I was just admiring your many calendars," Alice said, looking up at the ceiling.

"Ah, thank you," the man said. "I have quite a collection, you know."

"I see," said Alice. "But it seems you may have left out a month or two."

The man swallowed a bite of crescent and dabbed his mouth with a napkin. "Indeed," he said. "I've been looking for them everywhere. February of 1865 and February of 742. Once I find them, my gallery shall be complete."

"What I meant was ..." Alice began, then stopped herself, for she felt beginning a sentence thus was the surest path toward a nonsense conversation. "Why just February?" she asked, after giving the matter some thought.

29 Carroll had experience with sufferers of mental illness through his Uncle Skeffington's law practice. Carroll uses Multiple Personality Disorder here (although the disorder was not diagnosed until the mid 20th century, Carroll would certainly have been familiar with the symptoms) to further separate the personas of Dodgson and Carroll, the Dodgson one obviously the 'dodgy' one with the stammer that afflicted him most of his life.

"Why not?" the man said. "Never cared for the other months all that much myself. February is the only month I need, thank you. Has all twenty-eight days in it."

"But I'm sure there are months that do not have twenty-eight days."

"Nonsense!" the man said. "Every month has twenty-eight days in it. So if all of them have twenty-eight days, why not just pick a month you like and stick with it."

Alice could see there would be no convincing the man otherwise. "If I had to pick just one month and stick with it," she thought, "I suppose I should take December, for then it would always be Christmastime." She took one of the crescents, and nearly chipped a tooth on it, for it was harder than a stone.

"Such wonderful crescents," said the man. "These aren't the traditional shingling crescents, I'll have you know. These are the ones we toss at Jubjub birds, to frighten them out of the back garden."

Alice rubbed her sore jaw and tried to recall having seen a back garden to the tower. Then she realised that she couldn't recall having seen one because there hadn't been one there, and she told the man so.

"Quite right," said the man. "Quite right. Such an astute child! Very wise, indeed! That's why I keep a carpenter on staff at all times."

Alice was puzzled. "A carpenter?" she asked. "I should have thought a gardener would be in order."

"Oh, dear me, no!" said the man. "We already have a garden. Such a silly girl you are! Terribly thick-headed. No, no, we have the carpenter so that we might rearrange the tower whenever the Jubjub birds appear! It's his task to move everything in the front of the tower to the back, and everything from the back to the front. And the simplest way to accomplish that is to turn the tower itself around, of course. Only then can we go about scaring the Jubjub birds out of the back garden."

"It would seem to me," said Alice, who was still unsure what to make of being called brilliant and stupid in nearly the same breath, "that the most convenient thing to do would be to keep things as they are, and scare the Jubjub birds out of the *front* garden."

The old man chuckled. "Yes, you might think that. But it's been gone over any number of times, and that just wouldn't work."

"Why not?" asked Alice.

"Because," the man said, very slowly so that Alice might best understand him, "the Jubjub birds always land in *back* gardens. Everyone knows that. Even nobody[30] knows it." He smiled and patted her on the head. "Wo'n't you have some more tea?"

He extended the silver tray toward Alice, and she could see that his fingertips were stained with a dreadful black tincture. Still, the teapot and cups seemed clean enough, and she poured herself just a tiny bit.

30 Once again, Nobody appears – very likely the same Nobody Alice saw coming up the road, and who never gets executed in *Through the Looking-Glass.*

Chapter V.

Down and Up

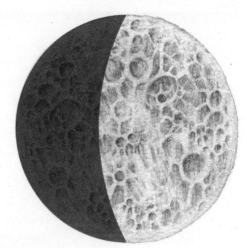

I t occurs to me," said the Man in the Moon (for Alice correctly deduced he could be no-one other), "that you might take some small enjoyment in viewing the gardens from my usual vantage point." And without explaining further, he put down his teacup, and walked over to a stairwell leading into the floor. He paused only a moment to beckon to Alice to follow, then disappeared below.

Alice was a bit disappointed, for she had yet to try her tea and was feeling very thirsty. However, when she looked into the cup, she found it was completely dry, except for some tealeaves clinging to the bottom. By an odd chance, they formed letters in the cup, and appeared to spell out HARD GRIEF.

"Hard grief?" she said. "I wonder what that means. Does it mean that grief is hard? That would scarcely seem to be new. Everyone knows that grief is hard. Perhaps there's more." Alice tilted the cup to see if there were more words in the cup, but when she did so, all the letters slid out of the cup and fell upside-down upon the floor. So, having no tea and no tealeaves, Alice took herself down the stairs.

The stairway took a great many twists and turns anti-clockwise, and all along the way Alice saw no sign of the funny old man. At each turn was a post, and in each post, Alice saw a different curious engraving. On the first post Alice saw a carving that looked like this:

ʼΑλιζ

Alice traced the carving with her fingers, feeling the indention into the column. "But what does it mean?" she thought.

As Alice continued on down the stairs, she found a carving at each level, only not quite so intricate as the one she had first encountered. On the second level, for instance, there was an **A**. After that, a **B**.

"Why, it seems to be the alphabet," Alice exclaimed, feeling rather proud of herself. But the next landing was marked with a stamped **Γ**, and the one after that with an embossed **Δ**, and so Alice decided the marks must be something quite different. And thus it went until Alice reached the last (and twenty-eighth[31]) twist in the stairs (which was marked with a carving the shape of which was **Ω**), where she finally caught up with the old man. He was looking wistfully out a window, his elbows resting on the sill and his enormous head in his hands. He turned and beamed at Alice when he heard her arrive.

"There you are," he said. "And about time, too. I've been waiting near on a month for you."

"It was an awfully long walk," Alice said by way of excuse.

"Fiddlesticks!" the man said. "It was merely

31 There are twenty-eight days in a lunar month. The tower seems to be a calendar of sorts.

a flight of stairs. I myself flew down them. You should try running down a helix, or crossing a lexicon! Then you would know what distance is.[32] But come! Here is what I wished to show you."

Alice came to him and, to her amazement, was able to view the entirety of the moon's surface through the window.[33] "Goodness!" she exclaimed. "Why, there's the mare I met when I arrived. She's fast asleep on the side of that hill. And there's the Queen – she looks none the happier, but I suppose having recently died will do that to a person. And there's the pink wood louse!" Alice leaned out of the window to wave to them all, but they were too far away and could not hear her. As she leaned out, she saw the brown wood louse, sneaking around a nearby hill hoping to catch the pink one unawares. "Oh dear, the pink one is in for another struggle, I fear. I do hope he has caught his breath back by now."

"I shouldn't worry about him," said the Man in the Moon. "No man has got past him yet[34]. And if one ever should, well, that person would be in for a nasty surprise!"

"Oh?" asked Alice. "There are other soldiers, then, protecting your palace?"

The old man beamed at her, and puffed his chest out so far that Alice feared he might fall over backward at the waist. "Archers," he said proudly. "On the roof, one for each direction. To the north, there is a bowman. To the south, there is a bowman. To the west, there is a bowman[35]."

"And to the east," Alice said, "I should suppose there is a bowman as well?"

"To the east –" the old man sighed wistfully. "Ah, to the east is where I was born.

32 Carroll's stairway is denoted on each level, it would seem, with a Greek letter. Given the description of its shape, it is a helix. It might be called a lexicon as well, due to its alphabetic markings. Dean Liddell is said to have named the main stairway in the deanery at Christ Church the Lexicon, after a Greek Lexicon he co-authored. There also may be some allusion to the phrase 'crossing the Rubicon', referring perhaps to the impending marriage.

33 What Alice doesn't notice is that she entered the structure on the ground floor, and has gone down, but now she looks out of the window as though she were at the top of the tower.

34 Of course, Alice got past him, but being a girl rather than a man, that would be logical.

35 Carroll is making a pun on the name of one of his closest child friends, Isa Bowman.

And I should like to be borne there again, some day. If you try very hard, you can see it from here."

Alice peered out of the window again, but no matter how hard she tried, she could see nothing more on the horizon, and eventually her eyes grew tired from straining. "I'm awfully sorry, but I just ca'n't make it out from here."

"Really?" the man asked. "Oh! But perhaps I have a picture! Wait for me here." And he set off up the stairs again.

Alice continued looking and, for a brief moment, thought she saw a silver twinkle just beyond the horizon.

"Oh! Do come quick!" cried Alice. "I believe I saw it!"

"Where?" She heard the man's voice, but it seemed to be coming from outside. She leaned out of the window and looked about, and there was his enormous pate, poking out of a window several levels below her. He shaded his eyes with one hand and squinted. "I don't see anything."

"It's – it's gone now, and I came all this way to find it" said Alice. "It was only there for a second."

The man shook his head sadly. "'twere ever so," he said. He pulled his head back inside, and was coming back down the stairs before Alice could even turn all the way around.

"Ah me, I couldn't find it," he said. "No matter. A picture is worth a thousand words, and I doubt a girl of your size has more than four-hundred and eighty-seven words in her, so there would hardly be room for an equitable exchange." He pulled up a little stool and settled himself upon it. "So then," he said, "you came here seeking what caused that flash of light? Where were you when you first saw it?"

Alice set about describing her home, and her sisters and mother and father, and her little white cat, and how the adults had all gathered to view some astronomical event with the telescope. She went on for a great deal longer than necessary, she felt, saying much of nothing ("Which is not nearly like a tiny bit of something, though almost – but not quite – just about equal to a little of not anything," she thought to herself as she spoke), until she finally got to how she had seen the sparkling flash on the moon and had used the telescope to bring it closer to her (or perhaps the other way about).

The old fellow nodded and rubbed his chin thoughtfully the entire time, hanging on Alice's every word, until she completed her tale.

"Very interesting!" he said, when she had finished. "Quite impossible, of course, and no doubt a very intricately contrived pack of lies, but very interesting nonetheless!"

Alice took offence at being called a liar, but wisely held her tongue, for the old man said it in such good humour that she could not be sure whether he had said "pack of lies" or "paca flies." (The latter was quite improbable, she realised, but possible, and Alice thought it best to give an elder the benefit of the doubt.)

The old man rose from his chair. "Well, this is all well and good, but I fear you could chat away an entire year and never find your way to Babylon."

"But do you have any idea as to how I might get home?" Alice asked, for she had no interest in seeing Babylon (at least not just at this moment) and surely someone must be looking for her soon, and Miss Prickett was always telling her to come down from high places. ("And how old Pricks will be cross when she finds me as high as the moon!" Alice thought.)

"Answers," the old man said. "Answers, you seek. No, no, I have no answers. I don't think such an answer is humanly possible. But that doesn't necessarily mean there isn't one! It only means we have to find an answer that's inhumanly possible!" And, quite distractedly, he left the room through a door that Alice hadn't noticed before, and she felt it best to follow.

Chapter VI.

An Illogical Device

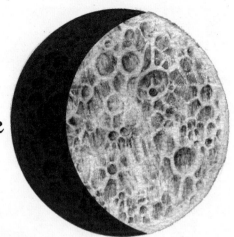

The room was the most cavernous expanse that Alice had ever been in, filled bottom to top and wall to wall to wall with the most curious of contraptions. Little globes of glass hung from the ceiling and glowed so brilliantly that Alice thought each must have contained a thousand fireflies. A strange machine sat off to one side, growling and worrying the bit of carpet it stood upon as though it were going to eat it all up. Bats flew in circles at the highest point of the room, little clockwork keys sticking from their backs.

"What wonders they have here on the moon!" said Alice. "When I get home, I shall surely be considered well travelled for the strange things I have seen."

In the middle of the room sat a large ramshackle box, with all manner of shuttered windows. A piano was mysteriously married to the box, and pipes grew from the top so tall that Alice was sure there wasn't a sweep in all of Oxford that would dare climb them.

"It's called an exwisedarium!" the old man proudly announced.[36] "It's an illogical machine."

36 In 1869, William Stanley Jevons invented the 'logical machine', also known as an 'abecedarium'. This was the first machine that could solve a logical problem faster than a person not using the machine. It was about three feet tall, and consisted of keys, levers, pulleys, and letters that could be either visible or hidden. When the operator pressed keys representing logical operations, panels would reveal the appropriate letters to show the result. Carroll, a collector of bizarre and unusual items may not have owned one, but he would very likely have been familiar with the device.

"An illogical machine," said Alice. "Whatever is it for?"

"Why, for producing illogic," he said. "I should think that would be obvious! It saves hours of time when making decisions of great importance."

Alice had to admit that she could see no reason for purposely producing illogic, especially when the results were to be applied to something important, and said so.

"Say, for instance, one considered building a meatsafe atop a church[37]," he said. "Now, the *logical* person might say that such an attempt is an exercise in nonsense, but such people are seldom those in positions of authority. No, the people in charge are more likely than not the ones who excel at *illogical* decisions, and even then they make so many so often that they find they need extra help to expedite their indecisions. Thus," – and he made an exaggerated flourish with his arms – "the exwisedarium!"

"It doesn't seem as that would be very intelligent," said Alice. "I mean, if it produces illogical advice."

"Precisely," he said. "Such an astute child! It's not intelligent. It's unbrilliant. It's exwise!"

Alice felt there was an argument to be made that a thing could be considered neither unbrilliant nor exwise unless it had been either brilliant or wise at some prior time – and she seriously doubted this contraption had ever been either – but, quite wisely, held her tongue.

"Observe," the man said, as he set furiously about the machine, pounding at the piano-like keys. Panels slid back and forth, covering and

37 Carroll refers here to the belfry being built at Christ Church during the 1870s. In his *The New Belfry of Christ Church, Oxford*, he states: "The word 'Belfry' is derived from the French *bel*, 'beautiful, becoming, meet,' and from the German *frei*, 'free, unfettered, secure, safe.' Thus the word is strictly equivalent to 'meatsafe,' to which the new Belfry bears a resemblance so perfect as almost to amount to coincidence." *The Complete Works of Lewis Carroll*, ed. Alexander Woollcott, London: The Nonesuch Press, 1939.

uncovering printed letters in combinations as to pose (or so Alice presumed) the question of the meatsafe on the church. The machine made beastly noises, and emitted a great cloud of dust and soot, sending them both into a fit of coughing.

"I'm so sorry about that," the aged man said, waving away the dust cloud around him with his hands. "My manservant, Hattah, hasn't been in to clean this room for some time." He smoothed the dust away from the keys, and began again. The machine blew out no clouds this time, but sounded no less beastly than before.

As he played at the keys, the aged man began to croak a little song, even less tunefully than the instrument:

Now that I'm in older days[38]
Still I swell with great emotion
Taking pleasure finding ways
Coaxing creatures from the ocean.

If perchance I trap an eel
On some sunny seaside foray
Such a joy inside I feel:
Molto Bene! Il Amore!

Here he began to pound the keys even harder. The exwisedarium rattled and shook, and steam whistled from the seams. Alice, fearing the machine might very well explode, crouched behind the table and covered her ears.

If some oysters I espy,
On their shells I'll rightly seat them.
If their names they do deny

38 The poem Carroll parodies here is from Isaac Watts' *Divine and Moral Songs for Children*, a source Carroll used more than once (see 'How Doth The Little Crocodile' and 'Tis The Voice Of The Lobster'.) This particularly lengthy piece espouses the moral of good intentions, and originally went like this:

Though I'm now in younger days,
Nor can tell what shall befall me,
I'll prepare for every place
Where my growing age shall call me.

Should I e'er be rich or great,
Others shall partake my goodness:
I'll supply the poor with meat,
Never showing scorn or rudeness.

Where I see the blind or lame,
Deaf or dumb, I'll kindly treat them:
I deserve to feel the same,
If I mock, or hurt, or cheat them.

If I meet with railing

Then I'll scoop them up and eat them![39]

If I meet with whaling lads
Why should I go with them whaling?
On my stretch of beach are scads
Of oysters got without my sailing.

When I see their gentle eyes,
Blinking, sparkling, gleaming, staring,
Salmon patties I'll devise –
So I sha'n't run out of herring.

When the perch perch out of reach
And the flounder flounder badly,
I'll presume it's time to teach
Young crustaceans to come gladly.

Said one lobster, "There are laws!
Contracts signed! Good sir, have pity!"
Ah, but it's those meaty claws
That, in butter, are so pretty.

With the lobster I'll contend
That the matter is contended.
If he asserts it's all pretend,
I'll submit the pot's pretended.

Ever watchful I shall be
O'er my boiling and my frying
As to burn not them nor me.
"Cooked is burnt enough," they're crying.

Could it be the cod was right
When he called my tastes erratic,
Just because I take delight
In a plate of shrimp or haddock?

As the machine wheezed to a halt, the aged

tongues,
Why should I return them railing,
Since I best revenge my wrongs
By my patience never failing?

When I hear them telling lies,
Talking foolish, cursing, swearing,
First I'll try to make them wise,
Or I'll soon go out of hearing.

What though I be low or mean,
I'll engage the rich to love me,
While I'm modest, neat and clean,
And submit when they reprove me.

If I should be poor and sick,
I shall meet, I hope, with pity;
Since I love to help the weak,
Though they're neither fair nor witty.

I'll not willingly offend,

Nor be easily offended:
What's amiss I'll strive to
   mend,
And endure what can't be
   mended.

May I be so watchful still
O'er my humours and my
   passion,
As to speak and do no ill,
Though it should be all
   the fashion.

Wicked fashions lead to
   hell;
Ne'er may I be found
   complying;
But in life behave so well,
Not to be afraid of dying.

39 The Walrus was also fond of
scooping up oysters. Was the
Walrus another representation of
Carroll? Carroll often met little
girls on the beach, fully charming
them with stories and puzzles.

40 These would be the initials of
Henry Liddell, Giles Gilbert Scott
and G. F. Bodley – the supporters
and architect of the offending belfry.

man turned toward Alice. "Well, what do you think?" he asked. "Would you like to hear more?"

"Oh, I shouldn't wish to be shellfish," said Alice.

The man seemed a little disappointed, but was quickly distracted as the machine gave a final groan and rattle as it finished doing – whatever it was doing. The open panels displayed a curious assortment of letters.

"There, you see?" he exclaimed. "HL(GS)GB.[40] That's … Hilgisigib! The proper algebraic notation, I'm sure, for indicating that building such a meatsafe is a good idea and should be acted upon immediately."

"But can the machine tell me how to get home?" Alice asked, only slightly impatiently.

They both looked over at the great exwisedarium, which seemed to slump just a little.

"I fear the strain would be too much for it," the old man said, sadly. "These machines are quite useful, but, alas, I fear they are built only ever to answer one question."

Alice was about to express – with no little vexation – that if the machine could answer only one question, that question ought to have been the one she most wanted answered.

Just then, there came a great clamour at the nearest window. The pane of glass shattered inward. "Dash it all!" cursed someone just outside the window.

The old man stomped over to the window and, throwing the latch, forced it up (which Alice thought completely unnecessary, for really, the glass was all gone and the window could hardly become more open than it already was).

"You there!" he called out. "What's the meaning of this?"

The person outside leaned into the open window. He was a sad-eyed man with a funny little box hat[41]. He had in one hand a hammer, and in the other a dish of butter. "The Jubjub birds are back again," he said, morosely.

"Ah," said the old man. "Well, then, carry on! Carry on!" The carpenter retreated none too soon, as the old man was quickly slamming down the broken window, and nearly caught the poor fellow's fingers in it. "He's a wonderful carpenter, really," he said to Alice. "But he costs me such great pains."

There was a rapid bit of hammering outside, followed by someone's hollering "Ouch!" which was then followed by the sound of someone's falling off a very tall ladder and landing in bushes.

The old man sighed and threw open the window again. "Do try to be a little quieter," he shouted. "We have guests, and it's quite impossible to have a pleasant chat with all your hammering and shuttering.[42]"

The only response was another thud, which sounded remarkably like a hammer being thrown against the side of the tower. The room shook slightly, and bits of plaster rained down on them. The old man looked up and shook his head. "We'll be needing more ceiling wax to fix that," he muttered, then he closed the window again and turned about to look at Alice.

"You shouldn't still buh-buh-be here," the man said, his lips quivering with dismay. Alice looked about to see if someone else had entered the room. There was no-one there but

41 Reinforcing the earlier mentioned imagery of the Walrus, Carroll brings in the Carpenter.

42 Dr. James Hunt was Carroll's long-time speech therapist, and authored *Stammering and Stuttering: Their Nature and Treatment* in 1861. This leads to speculation that Carroll had Hunt in mind when composing the poem recited by Tweedledee in *Through the Looking-Glass*. Carroll gave John Tenniel the choices of 'carpenter', 'baronet' or 'butterfly,' since any would fit the meter. It was Tenniel who chose 'carpenter.'

herself and the Man in the Moon, but his countenance had altered to one of grave mortification. "Wh-why haven't you luh-luh-left, yet?"

"Why, I've been trying," Alice said. "I asked you not five minutes ago how I might get home."

"You asked me nuh-nuh-no such thing!" he said, petulantly. "I …"

And he looked about. "Oh, my ceiling! Oh, my window! Oh, my – my precious exwisedarium!" So saddened was he by the chaos surrounding him that he could do naught else but sit on the floor and weep great tears into his handkerchief. "You vuh-vicious child! Coarse thing! Such a rough, to cuh-come and vuh-vuh-vandalise my home this way!"

"I did nothing of the sort!" Alice said. "The carpenter broke the window and the ceiling. And you yourself broke the –" (Alice was so confounded that she found it quite difficult to pronounce exwisedarium without sputtering, and so she just pointed to the collapsed construction) "– that thing!"

"Oh, please duh-do not add puh-petty lies to your list of crimes," the old man said weepingly.

Alice had put up with just about enough of this rude treatment. "I must say, I'm not sure I care for the way you're acting right now," she said.

"Acting?" the aged man said, bounding to his feet cheerfully, with not a trace of tears anywhere to be found on his cheek. "Why, what ever do you mean? I'm not acting at all. But then, if you'd care to act, I have just the thing!" And he walked quickly into an adjoining room, with Alice close behind him.

"How extremely curious!" Alice thought. "It's as though I'd spoken with two separate people entirely. But I didn't. Did I? I don't recall seeing one leave and the other come in. But then, people appear and disappear so quickly here. I shall have to blink with only one eye at a time if I do not wish to be surprised by any more rapid vanishings."

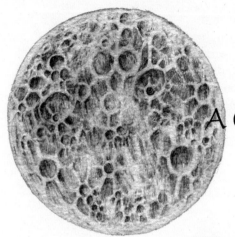

Chapter VII.

A Curious Stage Show

43   *Alice's Adventures in Wonderland* had been produced several times theatrically by this time, and Carroll had been heavily involved with each production.

44 Compare with:
All the world's a stage,
And all the men and
women merely players.
They have their exits
and their entrances;
And one man in his time
plays many parts ...
William Shakespeare, *As You Like It*, Act ii, Sc. 7

45 Among the many backyard amusements Carroll invented for his siblings (one of which was a mock train, complete with stations, schedules and refreshment booths) was a marionette theatre. The puppet plays he wrote and performed included one called *The Tragedy of King John*.

46 Carroll here refers to the *Alice's Adventures in Wonderland* stage play mentioned in footnote 43 – but it is the fictional Alice who has been on stage, not the real one.

The room was extraordinarily large, even larger than the one Alice had just left. This owed much to the fact that it had no roof, which afforded Alice a clear view of the star-filled sky. Lining the walls were several stages, each one adorned with curtains at either side, and each one set with unusual painted backdrops, ranging from outdoor spring settings to the insides of a sailing ship to a pasture of oversized mushrooms.[43] Dangling over each stage were several lengths of string, descending from so far up that Alice could not see from what they suspended.

"Every stage is a world[44]," the man said, slipping his wrists into one of the looped strings. "What shall we perform? I have them all, save the one about King John, which I lost in a fire. There's a tragedy[45], I can tell you! Come, come, surely you've been on a stage before?[46]"

Alice's parents, of course, would never deign to allow her to perform in such fashion, although she admitted that she had sometimes entertained her sisters by playing on the piano (although Alice's sisters would call such musical demonstrations entertainment only under the most extreme of tortures). But the man was bustling about with such energy that Alice was quite sure he was not listening to a thing she said.

"I shall be the Grand Dame, and you could be the principal boy," he said, excitedly. "Or you could be Joan and I could take the role of Mr Pulcinella.[47] But no, that would never do for strings, and I should hazard you haven't the head for it," he said, studying the base of Alice's neck. "But we could try it anyway if you like," he added with a hopeful enthusiasm. "We could begin in the middle, near the start but close to the end! Do you know the lines? 'Very well: then now, come, my turn to teach you.'[48]"

"Might we not do the one with the magical flute?" Alice asked, doing as he did and slipping the lowest hanging loops about her ankles before slipping the others over her wrists.

"Extempore!" he cried out. "There's the challenge! I'll be the dashing man of the world, Sir Roger Tichborne[49], Esquire, and you'll be the low and ugly pot maid, Mary Annette, who is secretly in love with him. Let's begin!"

And so having said, the man leapt into the sky, high as a house, then settled with a crash into a chair. "'Yeth; one of those things, like – why is so and so or somebody like somebody else,'" he said, his arms jerkily moving about.

"But I don't know this ... Oh!" And then Alice herself was yanked roughly into the air. She looked up the length of the wires, but could not see where they ended. Each one might as well have been tied off to a star.

47 *The Tragical Comedy, or Comical Tragedy, of Punch and Judy* (or Joan, as she was sometimes called), was a play for hand puppets. In it, Mr Punch kills all those who stand in the way of his adventure – including his wife and baby – often by knocking their heads off with a large stick.

48 Near the beginning for Mr Punch, but quite near the end for poor Judy, whose only lines that would follow this point in the play are to beg Mr Punch to stop hitting her with his stick, shortly before she dies. Alice, of course, *does* know the lines, and suggests a different play.

49 In 1873, Arthur Orton was indicted as an impostor for falsely presenting himself as Sir Roger Tichborne, heir to the Tichborne estates. Carroll was interested enough in the case to have telegrams sent to him regarding its outcome.

"How very curious!" thought Alice, as she descended back to the stage. "I wonder who it is pulling the strings?"

She landed on all fours beside the table, and was then jerked cleanly to her feet. A silver tray and decanter sat there.

"'Yeth, a drum,'" he went on, apparently heedless of Alice's difficulties. "'That's the idea. What is it gives a cold in the head, cures a cold, pays the doctor's bill and makes the home-guard look for substitutes? Yeth, do you give it up?'"

"Do I give what up?" Alice asked. Her wrists had become caught up in the lines and she was in the process of untangling them when she was suddenly jerked into the air once again.

"Well, I'll tell you – a draught. Now I've got a better one than that: When is a dog's tail not a dog's tail?" The man picked up his empty teacup and brought it to his lips, as though he were taking a full and hot sip of tea, placing the cup back on the table just as Alice came down on the other side.

"Oh!" she cried. Her wrists were now untangled, but her ankles were quite tied, the strings having caught on the buckle of her shoe, and she hung there upside-down while she wriggled trying to right herself.

"When it's a cart.[50]" he said, slapping his knee and laughing heartily.

"When what is a cart?" Alice asked. "Really, I'm having such difficulty here. Would you mind terribly – Gracious me!" cried Alice, as she was tugged yet again into the sky. Higher and higher she went this time, as the stage became smaller and smaller behind her.

"Come back!" the man called. "You'll miss

50 The lines recited by the Man in the Moon are those of the character Lord Dundreary in Tom Taylor's play, *Our American Cousin*. The last riddle is later explained when the ladies to whom it was told realise that Lord Dundreary used the word 'cart' when he meant 'wagon' (wagging).

the harlequinade! Oh dear, oh dear!

"Guh-guh-go on then," Alice heard him say next. "Guh-good riddance! Oh, my puh-poor house."

"Well, at least they can talk to each other, now I've left," said Alice as she soared upward. "He's certain never to be lonely when he has himself for company, even if his companion is such a dreary and disagreeable character."

Chapter VIII.

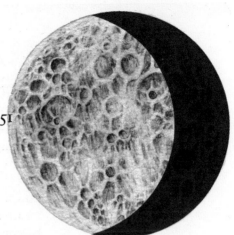

Hayah and Hattah[51]

A lice was set down in the middle of a long hall, the strings that carried her melting away as though they had never been there.

"So many doors!" said Alice, as she peered down the long hallway. "I wonder if I'm still in the Man in the Moon's tower?"

She began to walk the length of the hallway, peeking behind doors as she went. In one room she saw row after row of books. However, there was such a tumult going on inside, with wild orang-utans throwing chairs and statuettes all about, that Alice wondered how anybody could ever get any reading done in such a place.[52]

The next room was a music room, full of instruments – a piano, several violins, and various configurations of horns and strings such as Alice had never before seen. Sitting at each was a little person, playing each one furiously. Or so it seemed, for despite the great energy each performer put into his efforts, Alice heard nothing! It was as though her ears had suddenly become stopped with cotton. She couldn't even hear her own footsteps until she had moved away from the room!

51 There can be little doubt that these two are the Mad Hatter and the March Hare. The pair repeated their appearance from *Alice's Adventures in Wonderland* in *Through the Looking-Glass* as Haigha and Hatta. This chapter features probably the most direct connection the author has made between 'lunacy' and 'lunar'.

52 Carroll may be making a reference here to the 'Library Riot' of 1870. On May 10, students broke into the Christ Church library in protest over the dismissal of a porter named Timms. The break-in resulted in the damage of several busts and statuaries, which were tossed on a bonfire.

The hallway went on forever, an endless parade of doorways that each opened upon a scene more bizarre than the last. "I must be in a museum of sorts," Alice thought, as she passed a doorway through which she could see a number of worms, each as tall as she, standing about a table and peering at an array of maps spread out in a messy clutter. One of the worms had a helmet strapped on and made several thoughtful pronouncements about "munitions" and "supply lines" and "fine weather for it, if you ask me" as the other worms all seemed to nod in agreement.

At length, Alice reached the end of the hall, at which there was a door that was extremely tall but extremely narrow, and she had to turn sideways twice before she could squeeze through it.

The kitchen (for that was where Alice now found herself) was in sore need of a good cleaning. Every surface was covered with precariously teetering towers of dirty pots and pans. The forks and spoons lay in a basket on the floor, completely ignored, while Hattah (for that was whom Alice found herself with) sat at the long table, his head resting forlornly in his hands.

"Wash us," the spoons cried.

"Save us," the forks entreated.

"Be quiet!" Hattah screamed, and threw a dirty ladle into the basket with such violence that Alice was quite sure the cutlery would be damaged.

Hayah (for that is whom else Alice found herself with) sat on a very tall stool beside the great oven. He held a cup of tea in one hand and a piece of bread-and-butter in the other. However, he held them with the greatest of difficulty, for upon each of his hands was a large padded mitten. As a result, the tea sloshed sloppily over the edges of the cup, while the bread-and-butter had been mashed into a most unappetising appearance.

"Is it done, yet?" Hattah demanded. "Speak, wo'n't you?"

Hayah reached in his waistcoat for his pocket watch (spilling as he did so his teacup, which fell to the floor with a great crash) and held it up by the fob. (This took a great number of attempts and was accomplished only by Hayah's also dropping the ball of bread-and-butter to the floor so that he could snatch at the dangling watch with both mittened hands.)

"Five o'clock," he said. "Nearly done."

"It was five o'clock when you put it in," Hattah said.

"That was a different five o'clock," Hayah said simply. "This is a much later five o'clock than that one."

"When will what be done?" Alice asked, not sure what it was they were all waiting for, but feeling very uncomfortably like an eavesdropper without participating in the conversation to some degree.

"The pie! The pie!" Hattah shouted. "Oh! I shall die of hunger if I do not eat soon."

"Ah," said Alice, knowingly (and although she was still very much ignorant of what the two were discussing, she felt that she could say at least that much knowingly, since she did know there was a pie involved in some fashion). "I love pie. When will it be finished?"

"At five o'clock," said Hayah firmly. "And not one minute after."

"But could it very possibly be done one

minute before?" Hattah asked, hopefully.

"I don't see why not," said Hayah, who hopped down from his stool and opened the oven door. Great roils of smoke poured from the oven. Hayah reached so deeply inside it that Alice was quite sure the slightest nudge would have made him fall into it. ("Just like that old witch in 'Hansel and Gretel'," thought Alice, although she was far too nice to ever consider pushing anyone into an oven. She thought she saw a mischievous glint in Hattah's eyes, but Hayah pulled himself from the oven before Alice was quite certain of Hattah's intentions.)

"There we go," said Hayah, holding the pie before him. His face was turned away from the pie as he carried it, and Alice couldn't quite blame him, for the smell reminded her of a fish she had once encountered having washed up on the beach, only now mingled with smoke and creosote. "All ready for the eating, easy as cake." He placed the pie upon the table, then rummaged about in the basket of cutlery for a serving-knife. He didn't find one. He did find a gardening-trowel, however, and cut a very tiny sliver from the pie. Then he cut another very tiny sliver.

"We shall have pie enough to feed an army at this rate," Hattah cried. "There are only the four of us."

"Which only goes to show how well you can count," said Hayah. "There's me. Then I. Myself included. You. Yourself. Hayah, Hattah, Dormouse." (Alice looked about for the Dormouse at the mention of his name, but saw him nowhere.) "Then there's Alice. She. Then he. Then you're he to Dormouse and he's you to me when I speak to him directly.

Why, I shouldn't be surprised if we don't have enough pie here at all!"

"Oh, just hurry up about it," said Hattah. "Slice it how you need, so long as I get mine."

And Hayah did continue slicing, each slice just as narrow as the slice before it, so thin that Alice could hardly tell it was a slice at all.

"How do you cut it so delicately?" Alice asked.

Hayah smiled at her as he cut the last and seventy-first[53] slice. "It's all a matter of degrees," said Hayah. "Fortunately, I possess many. I have a PhD, a DDM, an SPR[54], two ASNs, and a Kelvin award for my performances at Retortions and Mutterations."

"You might have done better, had you not slept through your Corrections[55]," offered Hattah.

"I was robbed," Hayah said beneath his breath, brandishing the trowel in a manner that Alice felt quite sure was an unsafe one. "That old know-it-all instructor spent the entire time glaring down at my ... Ah! There we go!" (Here he had finished the final cut and, with the flat of the knife, served it very carefully.)

Alice looked at the pie, as it oozed its brackish, gelatinous contents upon the plate. "It's a very interesting pie," she said as politely as she could without actually tasting it (by which point, of course, she had resolved she would not). "Whatever is in it?"

Hayah puffed out his chest and fumbled at his tie, the end result of which left it in even greater disarray than when he had started.

"He's quite proud of the recipe, you know," said Hattah. "It's been in his family for

53 In his diaries, Carroll writes of mnemonic devices he used for remembering numbers, one of which, he claims, allowed him to memorise pi out to seventy-one decimal places.

54 Carroll, a believer in psychic abilities, was a charter member of the Society for Psychical Research. Could this S.P.R. be a reflection of that? See 'Lewis Carroll and the Society for Psychical Research', R. B. Shaberman, *Jabberwocky* (Summer 1972).

55 It was the practice at Christ Church to test students each year with written and oral examinations. The second term ended with 'Responsions', and the second year with 'Moderations'. 'Collections' were written exams of great duration. When it came time for Carroll to do his Collections for Thomas Gaisford (the then Dean of Christ Church, who first implemented the Collections process), he was given "a single day in which to prepare the Acts of the Apostles, two Greek plays, and the entire Satires of Horace." *Lewis Carroll: A Biography.* Donald Thomas. 1996.

generations, and even a few years."

By this time Hayah had climbed upon the table to address his audience. He made a theatrical pretence at clearing his throat, clasped his hands in front of him, and repeated:

There is inside the pie[56]
An apple and a fig
Three pomegranates, two cups lye,
And fully half-a-pig.

Now mince them very fine
Then fold into the mix
Some wet collodion[57] and some twine.
Oh! What a pie we'll fix!

"Oh, he's making me hungrier," complained Hattah, licking his chops. He reached into the bucket and withdrew a spatula, then began tapping it loudly against the tabletop. Hayah, meanwhile, continued his recitation with greater energy.

Take care, don't spill a drop.
It wouldn't do to waste!
A queechy[58] coffin drapes the top.
Take laudanum and baste.

Bake three days with no heat.
Carve with a flensing knife.
A pie like this you'll never eat
Again in all your life![59]

By this time Hayah had capered dangerously close to the edge of the table, and toppled into Hattah's lap.

"Careful! Careful ... Oh!" cried Hattah,

56 Another of Isaac Watts' *Divine and Moral Songs for Children*. The original poem goes like this:
  There is beyond the sky
  A heaven of joy and love;
  And holy children, when
    they die,
  Go to that world above.

  There is a dreadful hell,
  And everlasting pains:
  There sinners must with
    devils dwell
  In darkness, fire, and
    chains.

  Can such a wretch as I
  Escape this cursed end?
  And may I hope,
    whene'er I die,
  I shall to heaven ascend?

  Then will I read and pray,
  While I have life and
    breath,
  Lest I should be cut off
    to-day,
  And sent t' eternal death.
It seems fitting that Carroll would lampoon this particular poem, given his earlier noted ideas regarding the concept of eternal punishment.

tumbling backward with Hayah atop. The dishes clattered noisily, several of them smashing on the floor. A teapot rolled on its side, and the sleeping Dormouse tumbled out of it.

"Goodness!" exclaimed Alice. "How can he sleep through such clamour?"

"He's been that way since last month," said Hayah, righting himself.

"Since the end of the month before," corrected Hattah, brushing himself off. "The whole month was quite mad for him.[60]"

"Hmmph! Mad for him," said Hayah. "Why, it was no less mad for me, and you don't see me sleeping like a … like a …"

"Dormouse?" ventured Alice.

Hayah gave her a contemptuous look, then continued. "Well, he has no right to sleep! I'm the one who travelled the world over last month! I ran with the bowls in Madrid, hunted boojums in Madagascar, bought plaid hats in Madras, built igloos in Madhya Pradesh …"

"Nearly drowned off the islands of Madeira," muttered Hattah to himself.

"Quite so!" said Hayah. "So if anyone ought to be able to lay claim to exhaustion, I should!"

The Dormouse rubbed at his whiskers and rolled over on the table. "My point exactly," he said, eyes still closed, as he tumbled off the edge of the table and into Alice's lap, where he continued to slumber soundly.

"Such a dear thing," Alice said, stroking the Dormouse's whiskers. "So soundly he sleeps." As she held it, she tried to recall a lullaby to sing to it:

My little dormouse fell asleep,
And would not wake for tea.

57 Wet collodion was the chemical used in the particular type of photography Carroll indulged in. A glass plate would be coated in the substance, placed in the camera, then exposed for a minute, before being removed and developed in pyrogallic acid.

58 *Queechy* was a novel by Elizabeth Wetherell (a pseudonym employed by Susan Bogert.) The story involved a little girl who loves a man old enough to be her father, whom she later marries. Carroll gave this book to his younger sister, Henrietta, on her twelfth birthday. A 'coffin' is the top crust of a pie.

59 Given the poisonous nature of some of the ingredients, Hayah is most likely correct!

60 If the story occurs in August, Hattah is telling us then that the dormouse had a 'Mad June'. Madjoon is a Turkish word for opium.

He dozed and dozed for weeks and weeks,
But soon he'll wake for tea.
He'll clean his face and whiskers neat,
And then shall have his tea.[61]

"At least, I think that's how it goes," said Alice. "Did I get the words all right?"

But neither Hattah nor Hayah could answer her, for they had both fallen quite asleep, their heads resting comfortably on their folded arms. Alice gently lifted the Dormouse from her lap and laid it on the table between the two. Hayah snored loudly. The Dormouse shifted just a bit. "Treacle," it mumbled, before settling down once again into a deep slumber. Quietly, Alice left through the kitchen entrance and made her way along a winding downhill path.

61 The original poem is by Christina Rosetti, and reflects the high infant mortality rate of the period.

> Our little baby fell asleep,
> And may not wake again.
> For days and days, and
>   weeks and weeks;
> But then he'll wake again,
> And come with his own
>   pretty look,
> And kiss Mamma again.

Chapter IX.

Achilles and the Tortoise

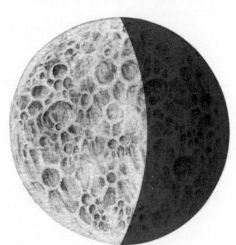

As she wandered, the path Alice followed slowly became overgrown with all varieties of blossoms. There were primroses and soapworts, all kinds of catchflies, and tuberoses in copious quantities. They grew so high that their tops bowed under their own weight, and they formed a canopy of dark leaves and luminous petals for as far down the path as Alice could see.

"Oh! What beautiful flowers!" Alice exclaimed. She stood on tiptoe and pulled a delicate tendril close to her nose, better to savour the heady scent. So taken was she with the scenery that she didn't notice the lunar moth[62] until it was right upon her.

"I would greatly appreciate it," said the moth in a gruff voice, "if you would cease your despoiling of my garden."

"I beg your pardon," said Alice, curtsying gracefully as she apologised. She noticed that the moth was dressed in gardening clothes. It held a spade in one hand, and a watering can in the other. "I don't think I damaged it," she added, rather doubtfully.

"You don't think," the moth grumbled. It

[62] The caterpillar that metamorphoses into a lunar moth is hairless and segmented, much like Tenniel's rendition of the caterpillar in *Alice's Adventures in Wonderland*. It is possible that Carroll intended the lunar moth to be a matured version of the classic hookah-smoking character, but there isn't enough evidence to do more than speculate.

made a fuss of straightening out the leaves where Alice had been standing, its wings quivering with annoyance. "You don't think," it said again. "There's an admission I shouldn't be surprised at hearing. What's your name, stupid child?"

"Alice," she said. "And I didn't mean to say that I don't think at all!"

"No, no, I'm sure you didn't," said the moth, now busily watering the leaves and stroking them as though Alice had treated them very roughly indeed. "Probably meant to keep it a secret, I shouldn't doubt. I'd certainly have kept it secret if *I* didn't think at all."

Alice opened her mouth to explain once again what she had really meant, but wisely decided the argument would continue to be turned against her. "If I could only find my way from the moon back to my home on Earth, I should gladly leave your beautiful garden."

"Then go home, Alice," it said. "You're only thirteen steps from Earth if you take the distance and double it up."

"He's mad," Alice thought to herself. "But then, so many strange things have happened to me here on the moon, that perhaps I ought to give it a try."

Alice walked away from the moth, who was muttering about his lost garden trowel. She counted steps as she walked. "One. Two. Three."

She had counted as far as twelve when she chanced upon a man done up in unusual armour, as though he had just returned from waging war in ancient Troy. More curious however (at least to Alice) was the armoured man's companion, who happened to be an enormous Tortoise.[63]

"Dear me," said Alice. "The moon is such a busy place. I'm sure I never suspected so many lived here."

"My dear friend, Achilles, and I do not live here, dear girl," said the Tortoise. He smiled pleasantly at her.

"Hardly," said Achilles. "We live in Ancient Greece. Or lived, rather. It's quite removed from where you come."

"By a small ocean and a few thousand years," the Tortoise chuckled.

"And did you come by telescope?" Alice asked.

"Telescope?" said Achilles. "What does she mean, friend Tortoise?"

"I think she's far-sighted," the Tortoise whispered back. "I, of course, divined that straight away."

"I should have been disappointed in you if you hadn't," said Achilles. "She must have forgotten her spectacles, poor thing."

"They might not yet have been invented," whispered the Tortoise.

Alice ignored their comments. "I merely wished to know how it is you arrived here."

"Well, why didn't you say so?" said Achilles.

"Perhaps she thinks she did," said Tortoise. "The younger ones always are that way, you know."

"Indeed," agreed Achilles. "Well, as it happened, my friend Tortoise and I had gone out for an evening stroll, stretching our legs for a race we were planning."

"He's going to give me a head-start, naturally," said the Tortoise to Alice, with a conspiratorial wink. "That will be his

63 Here we find the Tortoise and Achilles still engaged in discussion of the paradox of change proposed by the philosopher Zeno, who pitted the two against each other in a race that could never end to illustrate his idea. Carroll later used Zeno's characters in *What The Tortoise Said To Achilles*, published shortly before the author's death. In Carroll's narrative, the two discussed – at infinite length – Euclid's first proposition. This find indicates Carroll intended to use the two much earlier. *Mind*, No. 4, 1895, pp 278-280.

downfall."

"And we were admiring the moon," continued Achilles. "And I asked my friend if perhaps we could race there and back."

"Waiting, of course, until such time as the moon was on the horizon," said Tortoise. "But even then, I felt that such an undertaking was sheer lunacy."

"The moon was simply too far away, he told me," said Achilles.

"Too far by far," the Tortoise declared.

"And then my good friend Tortoise reminded me that not only could I never travel to the moon, under any conditions," said Achilles, "but that – for reasons I admit I still have trouble grasping – I could travel nowhere else, either."

"Why, that's nonsense," said Alice. "I travel all the time."

The Tortoise sighed. "I shall have to explain it to you both, I suppose," he said morosely. "Although I shall never get him to race me after this. Now consider: before you can go to some place, you must first go half-way there. You will grant me that, wo'n't you?"

"I certainly would," Achilles said.

Alice agreed that it made sense, for it seemed to her quite impossible to go all the way to any place without first going one half the distance.

"And before you can go half, you must first go half that, or one quarter of the distance, no? And before that, one eighth."

"Oh dear," said Alice. "I shall be needing pencil and paper to be doing such figures."

"You needn't bother," said Achilles. "It's all simple enough if you pay attention, and really, there isn't enough paper.[64]"

64 Carroll foreshadows his later paper, wherein Achilles fills an entire notepad and still hasn't transcribed all the steps the Tortoise dictates.

"True, true," intoned the Tortoise. "Now, do keep up." The Tortoise then expounded for nearly an hour, going through sixteenths and thirty-seconds, and four-million-one-hundred-and-ninety-four-thousand-three-hundred-and-fourths, until Alice was quite sure that the numbers could go no higher (or smaller, as the case happened to be).

"At any rate," Achilles interrupted ...

"At every rate ..." the Tortoise said. "You find you are unable to go anywhere at all."

"And thus, motion unexists. QED.[65]" The Tortoise folded his flippers across his chest smugly.

Alice considered this carefully. "It makes a kind of sense," she thought. "But then, I'm certain that I reach the places I set out to see. At least, most of the time."

"Are you quite certain?" Achilles asked.

"It's all imaginings," the Tortoise said. "Obviously you couldn't really go anywhere at all, as I've just proved, therefore you must go nowhere."

"But then," Alice asked, quite confused, "how did you get to the moon at all?"

"Diminishment," said the Tortoise.

"Do tell!" said an astonished Achilles.

"When one continues bisecting the distances, as we have done, one ends up with an infinite number of segments that are as close to zero as makes no odds, provided one rounds the numbers sufficiently."

"I do remember rounding them, now that you mention it," said Achilles. "We used a file, correct?"

"So many of them were square,[66]" said the Tortoise to Alice. "Regardless, an ocean of

65 Douglas Hofstadter explores this concept further in his Pulitzer Prize-winning book, *Gödel, Escher, Bach: An Eternal Golden Braid*, a thoroughly Carrollian treatment of minds and machines. NY: Basic Books. 1979.

66 In this, we must assume the Tortoise evaluates a total distance as '1'. Once the divisions begin, squares appear. 0.25 is the square of 0.5. Take any number from the natural progression, square it, and the resulting number is still a member of the sequence.

zeroes is still zero, no matter how many rocks you throw into it."

Alice remained silent, not wishing to say the wrong thing and be thought ignorant. "I've never seen a square number," she thought. "Four looks a bit like a square, and possibly eleven. And one hundred eleven, I suppose, or does that lean more toward being rectangular?"

"And, as it's as easy to go no distance once as it is to do so many times, we found ourselves here before Tortoise had finished his very eloquent argument," said Achilles.

"I daresay we arrived here before I even began it," the Tortoise offered graciously.[67]

"Indubitably," agreed Achilles.

Hoping to be helpful, Alice ventured that perhaps the pair might return by employing the same reasoning, only in reverse.

Achilles started at the idea, but the Tortoise only chuckled. "My dear, that was exactly what my good friend Achilles suggested upon arrival," he said. "Alas, upon the attempt, we were rewarded with nothing more than headaches. You just ca'n't divide it in reverse."[68]

"Nobody[69] gets anywhere that way," said Achilles.

"And he does so with such skill," the Tortoise agreed. "Would that we were he."

Alice was just about to ask them about the sparkling flash she had seen ("For surely two as wise as these must know just about everything there is to be known," she thought) and where she might go to find it, when, at that moment, a brilliant flash lit up the sky, followed by an explosive boom, both of which came from just beyond a ridge.

67 Carroll wrote in 1879 to one of his child-friends, Edith Blakemore, that he would sometimes go to bed the minute he awoke, and that sometimes he retired so early as to go to bed the minute before he awoke! *The Annotated Alice: The Definitive Edition*, Martin Gardner, 2000.

68 Since the Tortoise and Achilles arrived by multiplying the infinite number of sequences by zero, the reverse would require division by zero, a mathematical impossibility.

69 Another appearance by the multi-talented Nobody.

"NO GOAL! ZERO POINTS!" someone shouted from in the distance.

"What in the world was that?" Alice exclaimed.

The Tortoise yawned. "What in the world, indeed."

"How easily she forgets," said Achilles.

"What in the moon, rather," said the Tortoise.

"But to answer your question," said Achilles, "that would be the worms, playing at war again."

"War? But someone said something about points," said Alice.

"That was the referee," said the Tortoise.

"One ca'n't have a proper war without someone keeping score," said Achilles. "Otherwise how would one know when one had won? Or, for that matter, if two had, too?"

"You can get a better view of the proceedings," the Tortoise said, "from the vantage offered on that ridge, just over there." And he waved toward a rocky hill just behind Alice.

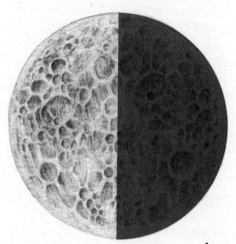

Chapter X.

The Worms
Have a Battle

A lice crested the ridge and saw a most extraordinary sight. Filling the entire valley below were giant worms, their segmented bodies armoured and outfitted for war.[70] There were great cannons being wheeled about, and muskets propped up with sticks ("For they have no hands with which to hold them," thought Alice). Each of them wore the exact same shade of grey, and appeared to Alice to be so uniform to each other that she wondered how they knew which worm fought for which side.

"They look very much like enormous earthworms," she said. "But then I suppose I shouldn't call them earthworms, should I? Perhaps they might be moonworms, then?"

"It's a grand battle they're raging tonight, isn't it?" asked a tiny voice beside her. Alice turned and was surprised to see that she was no longer alone on the ridge, but was in a rather large menagerie of spectators. The ant beside her was rubbing its hands together gleefully. "Best battle I've seen all year!"

"But what are they fighting over?" Alice asked.

70 The young Carroll not only made pets of such creatures as toads and snails, but also "tried to promote modern warfare among earthworms by giving them small pieces of clay pipe for weapons." *British Authors of the Nineteenth Century* (pp 119-121).

"Why, to win, of course!" the ant exclaimed. "What other reason is there to fight a war?" And it turned its attention back to the field, cheering loudly as the next blast dispersed a small group of worms that were advancing on the cannons.

Alice watched for a while, but soon grew bored with the display, and began eavesdropping on the other creatures about her.

"Did you know he could slice a pie like that?" a ladybird asked of the beetle next to her. "I never saw such a thing!"

"I just want to know what kind of spice he uses to bring out such flavours," the beetle replied. "I tried to duplicate the recipe on my own, but failed. He baked another today, you know. I think he does it just to spite me."

"You mean Hayah's pie?" asked Alice.

The two creatures looked at Alice disdainfully. "As though you've been to the Man in the Moon's suite to sample cookery as fine as his chef Hayah's," sniffed the beetle.

Alice wrinkled her nose. "Honestly, I didn't find his cooking that fine at all. Particularly that awful pie."

"Awful? Awful?" The ladybird was shocked. "Why, I'll have you know that, if it suits him, he can make puddings out of suets, and fine pastries out of newspapers!"

"Oh, do calm down, Mildred," the beetle said. "You're just overly excited because we arrived too late to hear the opening duets before the battle began. It's hardly the girl's fault if she doesn't appreciate the diets of those more cultured than herself."

"But to call Hayah's cooking awful," sputtered the ladybird. "It's unconscionable.

It cast all kinds of dirts upon his reputation."

"I know, it's the worst of all possible girts," the beetle said. "But there's no getting around the girth of some people's ignorance, so there's no point in getting all worked up about it."

The ladybird shook herself, then settled back down into her seat. "I suppose you're right, Millicent," she said (and Alice was very grateful, for she hadn't meant to offend at all). "Still, I'd have been much happier if she" – and she indicated Alice with a subtle tilt of her head – "would have stayed in the moth's garth[71] instead of spoiling our evening."

Alice sat on the ground quietly, her hands folded neatly in her lap. The ant beside her leaned over and patted her shoulder. "Don't mind them," it said, cheerfully. "I've been coming to these battles for years now, and they always seem to find something or someone that irritates them to no end. I think they enjoy it."

"Well, it's good to know I don't annoy all the creatures here," thought Alice. "But then, if they do like being irritated, and I irritated them, then wouldn't that mean that they like me as well? Oh, I do hope when I grow up that I shall continue to be irritated by irritations, and never come to enjoy them."

But Alice's thoughts were interrupted by the renewed commotion below.

"Fire!" shouted one worm commander. At his command, three other worms released a catapult that vaulted a great quantity of wretched slugs through the air. They flew well over their intended target, and would have landed quite on Alice, had she not run away at the very last moment.

71 The reader will notice that there is something odd about the conversation of the beetle and the ladybird, and that some of the words sometimes rhyme or near rhyme. The key is when the ladybird refers back to the moth's garth, or garden. The moth tells Alice she is only thirteen steps from Earth, if she would take the distance and double it. Or, in this case, doublet, a word ladder game Carroll invented wherein one word is transformed into another by changing one letter each time. Upon rereading, you will see that Alice does reach Earth in thirteen steps of a doublet, as follows: ALICE, SLICE, SPICE, SPITE, SUITE, SUITS, SUETS, DUETS, DIETS, DIRTS, GIRTS, GIRTH, GARTH, EARTH.

"ALICE   DODGED   THROWN SLUGS![72]" called the referee (and Alice could only guess that he held that position, for he was in appearance no different from any of the other worms). "FIVE POINTS!"

"Get her out of there!" yelled the worm that had given the order to fire the catapult. "Foul! Foul, I say!"

"Interference!" screamed the leader of the other army. "No fair!"

"I don't see what right they have to be so upset," thought Alice. "I'm the one they just nearly missed."

"It makes no difference," said the ant. "All is fair, and you should watch yourself, lest you find yourself engaged in matters beyond your ability to control."

"I don't see why I should have to become involved," said Alice. "It's their war, and I should like nothing to do with it."

The worms, meanwhile, were re-grouping, and seemed to have struck some sort of alliance, for suddenly cannons that were facing each other were now all pointed toward the crowd (and, more specifically, at Alice!)

"Oh, oh, oh!" cried the ladybird, trembling. "We're done for! Oh, you wicked child! Now we shall all be quite late! The worms are turning on us!"

Alice, who wasn't a bit frightened of anything that an army of worms might do, was still taken aback by the ladybird's suggestion. "Surely they don't mean to attack us!" she thought.

But surely they did! The referee was shouting and squirming about, trying to put the war back on its proper course, but the two leaders were having none of it.

72 The referee's pronouncements are all anagrams. In this case, CHARLES LUTWIDGE DODG-SON.

"Fire!" shouted the one.

"Pull!" shouted the other.

There was a burst of light accompanied by a deafening explosion! Suddenly Alice (and the ladybird, and, indeed, the entire crowd) was pelted by a great quantity of rocks. They were very soft rocks, to be sure, and they hurt no-one in the least. Still, she was quite cross to find herself the target of these creatures, and stood up to give them a proper scolding.

The two worm leaders (and all the worm soldiers) were suddenly all a-tremble when they saw Alice stand, and squirried (which is a sort of movement that can be made only by frightened worms, and is a cross between a squirm and a scurry) away behind a makeshift wall of stones and cheese wheels.

"You should hide," said Alice. "It's quite impolite to throw stones at people, and I mean to show you why!" And, so saying, she picked up some of the rocks and hurled them back in the direction of the worm armies. Her throw was a very good one, and the rocks struck the rock fort[73] viciously, crumbling it.

"ALICE THROWS ORE THRU WALL![74]" the referee called out. "NO POINTS!"

The worms were in complete disarray, and writhed over each other in a heap. Several of the spectators were leaving, grumbling that such behaviour was terribly unsportsmanlike, and that they missed the days of simpler games like chess or croquet. The others glared at Alice, and for a moment she was concerned that they might all be very upset with her, and that perhaps she ought to apologise and take her seat.

Just then a great darkness began to fall, as

73 If the shelter is made largely of cheese, might the rock fort not be made out of Roquefort?

74 LEWIS CARROLL, THE AUTHOR.

though night came without the courtesy of twilight. Alice looked up in time to see a monstrous crow descending upon them all, its feathery wings as black as pitch. ("Like a tar barrel," thought Alice.) The worms screamed and wriggled as the crow descended, its great wings slowly spreading wider and wider until nearly the whole of the moon was enveloped in inky darkness.

"ECLIPSE CALLED, AN' ALL DIE![75]" yelled the referee, as calmly as ever, despite the panic all about him. In fact, he remained resolutely calm right to the very end, when the crow picked him up in its beak and ate him.

75 A final anagram: ALICE PLEASANCE LIDDELL.

Chapter XI.

A Very Long Fall

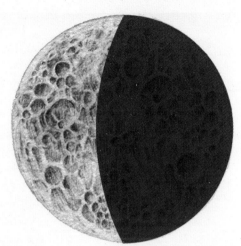

Alice tumbled through the darkness. It was a very curious sort of darkness, for while all about her was black, she could see her own self quite clearly, as well as several other creatures falling alongside her, including (to name only those nearest to her at the time) a bat, a crow, and a cow.

"Well," she thought, "at least I'll not be alone as I fall to my death."

"What ever makes you think that is where you are falling to?" said the crow[76]. At least, Alice thought it was the crow, for the bird hadn't moved its beak in the slightest. Nevertheless, there was an overall sort of crow-ness to the voice she heard.

"Are you the same crow who just ate the army of moonworms?" Alice asked.

The crow looked at Alice, then peered suspiciously to its right, and then its left. It made a strange little belching noise, and Alice heard its voice again.

"Not I," it said. "And besides, who ever heard of moonworms? I'm certain such creatures do not exist." Which at the moment was very true.

76 Like the caterpillar in *Through the Looking Glass,* the crow seems to be able to read minds, and further, project its thoughts.

Further they tumbled. The bat, its wings flailing limply behind it, looked impatiently at Alice. "It seems to me," the bat said after a few moments, "that the polite thing to do while tumbling towards one's death with others, would be to have some pleasant conversation. That's my opinion."

"But the crow just said we weren't going to die," said Alice.

"The crow said nothing of the kind," said the bat. "Crows don't talk, you know."

Alice thought perhaps the bat hadn't heard the crow, although she seemed to remember from somewhere that bats had extraordinarily keen hearing. "Well, perhaps he was listening to something so far away that he couldn't hear things close up just then," she thought. The crow only winked at her.

"Where I come from," Alice said, "bats don't talk. In fact, no animals talk at all, except for mynah birds and parrots and sometimes a raven."

The bat shrugged its wings and looked mournfully downward. "It sounds like a dreadfully uninteresting place to call home," he said. "To have so many things running about that cannot converse. You should find dying quite a refreshing change, I should think."

"Just the same, I should prefer to go on living," said Alice.

"Not I," said the bat. "I've waited my whole life for this. Took me a lifetime to get here. I plan to enjoy it after working so hard to achieve it."

The crow cocked his head to Alice, and she heard it again. "Perhaps you're not falling at all," it said.

"Not falling?" Alice asked.

"Of course we're falling," said the bat. "Do you see ground beneath your feet? Do you feel wind rushing past your – I suppose you must call those things on the side of your head 'ears'?"

The crow cawed once, flapped its wings, and then began falling in an entirely different direction, sideways to the rest of them, until it was quite out of sight.

"Hmph!" said the bat. "Good riddance, if you ask me. I can't stand crows – they're absolute murder when it comes to good conversation, prone to all manner of unkindness."

"He didn't seem to be such a bad crow," said Alice.

"Not even as much as a 'good-bye' before he ... before he ..."

"Flew away?" Alice ventured.

"Yes, before he flew away," the bat muttered, looking curiously at his own wings. He flapped them once, which held him aloft for just a second, then continued falling with Alice and the cow.

"Do you suppose," the bat asked, hesitantly, "that I might be able to perform such a thing?"

Alice didn't see why it couldn't. "Bats fly all the time where I come from," she said.

The bat sighed. "Such a wonderful, glorious place it must be, where creatures can soar through the air." It stretched its wings again, flexing them.

Alice thought to suggest that not every creature could fly, but the bat seemed so blissful at the prospect that she couldn't bear to tell him.

"You wouldn't mind terribly, would you?" it asked.

"Not at all," said Alice.

The bat stretched its wings to their fullest and began to glide away. It paused but a moment to glide back to Alice, and saluted her by touching its taloned claw to its forehead. "Good-bye," it said, and, in a twinkling, it was gone.

"So bats do twinkle[77]," Alice said. "I suppose it's just the two of us now," she added, directing her attention to the cow, which, until now, had been pleased to say nothing.

The cow chewed its cud in silence for a moment before acknowledging Alice. "I'm not falling either," it finally said.

"You're not?" asked Alice. "Surely you don't mean to tell me you're flying as well? I was unaware that farm animals knew how to fly."

The cow shook its head. "Some fly, but only the ones that have wings, such as chickens and ducks and pigs."

"Pigs?" asked Alice.

"Of course," said the cow. "But only the ones that have proper wing structure. They flutter all around whenever the climate is about to change. Surely a girl of your age has heard of weather-pigs?[78] But to your point, no, I am not flying. I am merely in the middle of a very long jump."

"Over the moon!" Alice exclaimed. "I've heard of your feat!"

"Technically, they're hooves, not feet," said the cow. "And yes, they are quite powerful to propel one of my meatiness to such heights."

"They would have to be, I suppose," said

77 "Twinkle, twinkle, little bat," as the Mad Hatter recited.

78 As the Walrus said to the oysters, "... and whether pigs can fly."

Alice.

"Tell me," the cow said, thoughtfully, "how it is you heard about my jumping prowess?"

Alice straightened herself and folded her hands in her lap – a feat in itself, falling as she was – and repeated:

Hey Diddle Diddle
The cat and the fiddle
The cow jumped over the moon.

"Ah, so that's how it's been reported," the cow said.

"There's more," Alice offered, helpfully.

"Do tell? Pray, continue."

Alice cleared her throat and did so.

The little dog laughed to see such sport.

"How dare he!" the cow exclaimed (although she exclaimed it in such gentle tones that Alice wondered if the creature ever did anything otherwise than contentedly). "I shall see to it that I land on his tail."

And the dish ran away with the spoon,

Alice said, finishing her own tale.

"I'm not surprised," the cow said. "Oh, the dish means well, I'm sure, but he's too enamoured to realise that spoon is no ladle."

They continued to fall in the darkness, the cow chewing lazily and looking about, not in the least disturbed by the lack of ground beneath them. "It occurs to me," it said, finally, "that if one were, perhaps, to climb aboard my back, then one could land with me when my jump is completed."

"Oh! Thank you very much. That's very kind of you," Alice said.

The cow munched some more. "Not at all," it replied. "Come aboard." And Alice endeavoured to fall toward the cow. But the creature was just out of Alice's reach.

"You'll have to fall faster," the cow said, "if you wish to climb upon me." But no matter how hard she tried, Alice was not able to fall any faster than she was falling; which was very frustrating, for the cow seemed to have no such trouble at all, and the distance between Alice and the cow continued to grow.[79]

"Hurry!" the cow called. "I've reached the zenith of my jump and am going back down now!" But it was in vain, and the cow began to fall away from Alice faster and faster until, finally, Alice was all by herself.

Suddenly, there was a great tumult of voices, and Alice found herself falling past all manner of people and creatures. There were kings and queens and courtiers, decked out as playing cards or attired as chess pieces, all waving at her as she fell past them, falling themselves. Alice thought she saw a hatter and a hare, holding hands and spinning about in the air. But when she looked again, it was instead two Anglo-Saxon messengers. By the time Alice was nearly out of sight of them, she was convinced it was neither hatter nor hare nor messengers, but the cook and manservant from the Man in the Moon's tower.

Farther she fell, and faster. She passed by a white rabbit wearing a waistcoat, a lion, a unicorn, and two chubby twin boys. Turtles and tortoises – Gryphons and Greek warriors. All of them smiled and waved, although Alice

79 Carroll was, of course, familiar with Galileo's experiment that two objects falling together would fall at the same rate – a physical law to which the fantastic cow is apparently not bound.

couldn't help feeling that they all looked just a little sad. And as she passed them, they sang a sad little song:

> The blaze of noonday splendour,
> The twilight soft and tender,
> May charm the eye; yet they shall die,
> Shall die and pass away.

> But here, in Dreamland's centre,
> No spoiler's hand may enter,
> These visions fair, this radiance rare,
> Shall never pass away.[80]

Alice fell so far and so fast that soon she had passed by all the strange things, and then found herself all alone in the blackness.

"I suppose I shall continue falling for ever," thought Alice. "Which isn't such a bad thing, I suppose, for I'm sure I shouldn't wish to be stopping now."

And then –
– the
most
curious
thing –
– happened!

As she fell, Alice slowly turned heels over head. Suddenly she perceived she was no longer falling but was, rather, flying[81], ever upward – higher and higher – like a bird, or a bat, or an angel.

80 This poem is an original by Carroll, which he claimed came to him in a dream. It was written in 1882, and caused some re-evaluation on when this story was written. It seemed obvious at the beginning that Carroll was writing near the time of the Alice's marriage in 1880. Yet Collingwood places this poem squarely in 1882. Perhaps Carroll used the verses in this story, shelved them, and then reused them later, as he seems to have done with the Tortoise and Achilles?

81 Compare to the Queen's statements in Chapter 2. The late Douglas Adams, in his series *The Hitchhiker's Guide To The Galaxy* also described flying as the result of "throwing oneself at the ground and missing." He also had a thing or two to say about the number 42.

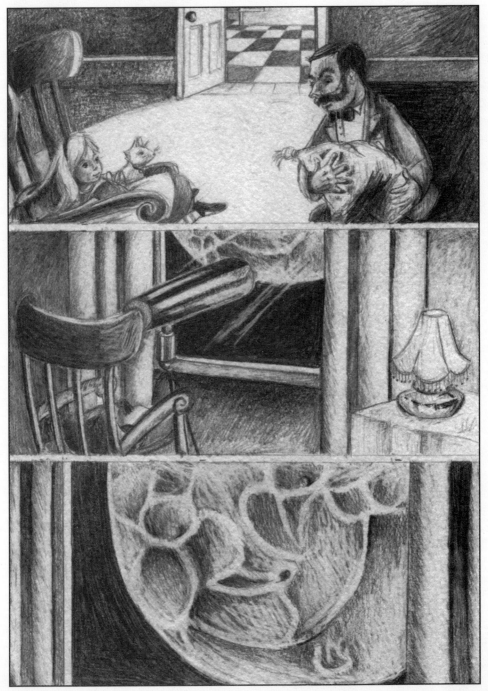

Chapter XII.

Down to Earth

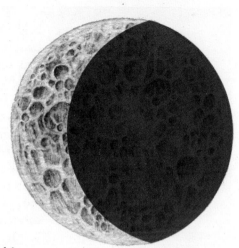

How long Alice floated she could not know, for there were no clocks falling alongside her by which she could tell the time. Presently, however, she began to hear more voices, as though there were a polite little party going on in just the next room ("If," Alice thought, "I were in a room for there to be a next room to this one. Which there may be, I suppose, provided this is nothing more than an extraordinarily enormous room that goes on for miles and miles. Wouldn't that be grand, if all the world were just one big room?")

The voices grew louder, but remained muffled, as though someone were holding a pillow over the entire party so that their words couldn't come all the way out.

And as she flew onward, she suddenly stopped! She had bumped her head against something very soft and very cushiony. "This must be the ceiling," said Alice. "Or the floor. Or quite possibly one of the walls," for she really had no sense of the direction in which she had been travelling.

Suddenly the room was suffused with

brilliance, and Alice looked up into the face of her father. He was lifting a pillow off her head, and she was astonished to find that she was curled up in the big parlour chair with Snowball nestled beside her (and looking quite annoyed at being awakened so rudely!)

"Alice, dear," her father said. "You really ought to wake up or you will miss the eclipse."

Alice rubbed her eyes, and saw that the grown-ups had reconvened, all gathered about the great telescope. She looked out of the window, but saw no sign of the moon.

"It really is gone," she said, sadly. "I wonder where the Man in the Moon will live now? And will he have to change his name? The Man in the Sky, perhaps?"

Her father chuckled. "Such nonsense you talk," he told her. "But here, see – the moon's quite all right. Take a look." And Alice peered through the telescope and saw the very first slivered crescent reappear as the great eclipse passed from it, as though the moon had been hiding behind a gigantic black curtain and was just now shyly and reluctantly peeking out to see if anyone had missed it.

"It's so bright," Alice thought, "as though it had just gone away for a bath. Perhaps this is what people mean when they talk about the new moon?" She pictured the Man in the Moon's poor carpenter rebuilding a replacement moon as quickly as he could from shiny new material.

Alice stepped away from the telescope so the other guests might look through it. But she continued to watch through the window as the moon continued to grow until it was once again a luminous white stone in the sky. Then, at her mother's urging, she gently picked up Snowball in her arms and carried her off to bed, stealing a piece of cheese from the serving platter as she passed it.

"The moon is really a wonderful place," she told the cat as she walked up the stairs, nibbling as she went. "There are such unusual things to see and do, and marvellous machines." Then she yawned, a deep, tired yawn. "But I shall have to tell you all about them in the morning, Snowball, for really, I am quite tired tonight. Perhaps I shall travel to the moon again someday, maybe when I have grown up. Which surely ca'n't be too far away, can it, as I seem to grow older each year. And the older I get, the more curious things seem to happen. Why, I imagine when I'm a woman, I shall have the most wondrous, fantastic journeys. I can hardly wait for that. And perhaps I shall take you with me, Snowball? Would you like that?"

But the cat merely raised its chin and purred as Alice scratched it a little, then jumped from her arms.

It was time for bed.

Benediction

Three lies now told,[82] a fancy wold
To which we may retreat,
Near hills and strands of fairylands
Through whimsical conceit.
And if by fate, past Heav'n's gate.
Each other we should meet –
Though Hell invade, thou wilt have made
My Paradise complete.

82 Contrast with *The Hunting Of
The Snark*: "What I tell you three
times is true."

Let light of reason not dispel
These vagaries chimaerical.

OTHER TITLES FROM TELOS PUBLISHING

TIME HUNTER

A range of high-quality, original paperback and limited edition hardback novellas featuring the adventures in time of Honoré Lechasseur. Part mystery, part detective story, part dark fantasy, part science fiction ... these books are guaranteed to enthral fans of good fiction everywhere, and are in the spirit of our acclaimed range of *Doctor Who* Novellas.

ALREADY AVAILABLE

THE WINNING SIDE by LANCE PARKIN

Emily is dead! Killed by an unknown assailant. Honoré and Emily find themselves caught up in a plot reaching from the future to their past, and with their very existence, not to mention the future of the entire world, at stake, can they unravel the mystery before it is too late?

An adventure in time and space.

£7.99 (+ £1.50 UK p&p) Standard p/b ISBN 1-903889-35-9

THE TUNNEL AT THE END OF THE LIGHT
by STEFAN PETRUCHA

In the heart of post-war London, a bomb is discovered lodged at a disused station between Green Park and Hyde Park Corner. The bomb detonates, and as the dust clears, it becomes apparent that *something* has been awakened. Strange half-human creatures attack the workers at the site, hungrily searching for anything containing sugar ...

Meanwhile, Honoré and Emily are contacted by eccentric poet Randolph Crest, who believes himself to be the target of these subterranean creatures. The ensuing investigation brings Honoré and Emily up against a terrifying force from deep beneath the earth, and one which even with their combined powers, they may have trouble stopping.

An adventure in time and space.

£7.99 (+ £1.50 UK p&p) $9.95 US $14.95 CAN Standard p/b
ISBN 1-903889-37-5
£25.00 (+ £1.50 UK p&p) $39.95 US $44.95 CAN Deluxe h/b
ISBN 1-903889-38-3

THE CLOCKWORK WOMAN by CLAIRE BOTT
Honoré and Emily find themselves imprisoned in the 19th Century by a celebrated inventor ... but help comes from an unexpected source – a humanoid automaton created by and to give pleasure to its owner. As the trio escape to London, they are unprepared for what awaits them, and at every turn it seems impossible to avert what fate may have in store for the Clockwork Woman.
An adventure in time and space.
£7.99 (+ £1.50 UK p&p) Standard p/b ISBN 1-903889-39-1
£25.00 (+ £1.50 UK p&p) Deluxe h/b ISBN 1-903889-40-5

The prices shown are correct at time of going to press. However, the publishers reserve the right to increase prices from those previously advertised without prior notice.

TELOS PUBLISHING
c/o Beech House, Chapel Lane, Moulton, Cheshire, CW9 8PQ,
England
Email: orders@telos.co.uk
Web: www.telos.co.uk

To order copies of any Telos books, please visit our website where there are full details of all titles and facilities for worldwide credit card online ordering, or send a cheque or postal order (UK only) for the appropriate amount (including postage and packing), together with details of the book(s) you require, plus your name and address to the above address. Overseas readers please send two international reply coupons for details of prices and postage rates.